Looks can be deceiving. . . .

"I called about the apartment. My name is Lisa Fontaine." She tucked a stringy strand of hair behind her ear. "If this is a bad time, I could come back later."

An embarrassed laugh escaped Isabella's lips. "Now is as bad a time as any."

Chewing nervously on her fingernails, Lisa seemed to study Isabella for a moment with her dull hazel eyes. "Do you want me to make you a cup of coffee or something?"

"Actually, that would be very nice."

Isabella's body began to relax. It was amazing how at ease she felt around Lisa. Even though she wasn't the type of girl Isabella usually hung out with, Isabella found herself chatting endlessly in her presence. *I've got a good feeling about this one.* She could feel it deep down in her gut.

"So when do you think you could move in?" Isabella asked.

"Really? I could do it any time," Lisa said eagerly. Then, suddenly, her face fell. "All my references are in New York. It might be kind of hard getting in touch with them."

"Never mind about that," Isabella said confidently. "I know a good roommate when I see one."

The *valley* has never been so *sweet*!

Having left Sweet Valley High School behind them, Jessica and Elizabeth Wakefield have begun a new stage in their lives, attending the most popular university around – Sweet Valley University!

Join them and all their friends for fun, frolics and frights on *and* off campus.

Ask your bookseller for any titles you may have missed. The Sweet Valley University series is published by Bantam Books.

SWEET VALLEY UNIVERSITY

THRILLER EDITION

The Roommate

Written by
Laurie John

Created by
FRANCINE PASCAL

BANTAM BOOKS
NEW YORK · TORONTO · LONDON · SYDNEY · AUCKLAND

THE ROOMMATE
A BANTAM BOOK : 0 553 50531 9

Originally published in USA by Bantam Books

First publication in Great Britain

PRINTING HISTORY
Bantam edition published 1997

The trademarks "Sweet Valley" and "Sweet Valley University"
are owned by Francine Pascal and are used under license by
Bantam Books and Transworld Publishers Ltd.

Conceived by Francine Pascal

Produced by Daniel Weiss Associates, Inc,
33 West 17th Street, New York, NY 10011

Bantam Books are published by Transworld Publishers Ltd,
61–63 Uxbridge Road, Ealing, London W5 5SA,
in Australia by Transworld Publishers (Australia) Pty Ltd,
15–25 Helles Avenue, Moorebank, NSW 2170,
and in New Zealand by Transworld Publishers (NZ) Ltd,
3 William Pickering Drive, Albany, Auckland.

Printed and bound in Great Britain by
Cox & Wyman Ltd, Reading, Berkshire.

To Taylor Leigh Grant

Chapter
One

_____

"Ready for your birthday present?" Danny Wyatt's dark brown eyes sparkled, and his handsome African American face caught the rich orange glow of the rising sun. Streaks of fiery colors stretched across the sky like fingers, spreading over Johnson Pond and beyond to the edge of the Sweet Valley campus.

Isabella Ricci turned her sleepy gray eyes away from the pond's glassy reflection and looked at Danny. "A present? But you've done too much for me already."

"It's not too much," Danny answered, his sensuous lips curving into a slow but serious smile. "I don't think it could ever be enough." He gently brushed Isabella's long black hair away from her face, pressing the palm of his hand against her creamy white cheek. "Now close your eyes."

1

Isabella obeyed without hesitation, listening closely to the faint rustle of Danny searching the pockets of his stylish sport coat. She pulled Danny's huge varsity jacket around her bare shoulders to ward off the cool wind that went through her strapless silk party dress.

This was one of the best birthdays I've ever had, Isabella thought dreamily, replaying the evening's events in her mind. It had started off with Danny taking her to a glorious dinner at El Capitano, the most expensive restaurant in town. From their table Isabella and Danny had had a perfect view of the blue Pacific, and after dessert they had taken a romantic stroll on the beach until it grew dark. Then Danny had whisked her back to campus, where he'd planned a surprise party for Isabella and all her closest friends. The three-story Theta sorority house had been absolutely crammed with people, and even Isabella was shocked to discover how many friends she had. The party had continued until the wee hours of the morning, when she and Danny had slipped out to the pond to watch the sunrise.

"This whole night has been incredible." Isabella sighed, her eyes still squeezed shut. "I can't imagine anything that could make it better."

Danny cleared his throat. "OK, Isabella—you can open them now."

Anticipation fluttered in Isabella's stomach

as she opened her eyes. Isabella noticed Danny's hopeful gaze as his strong hand stretched toward her. She saw a small blue ring box resting in his palm.

"Danny!" Isabella gasped. Her crimson lips quivered and her heart pounded as she stared down at the box. *This is it!* she thought between shallow breaths. *This is the moment I've been waiting for my whole life.* As a little girl Isabella had spent countless hours imagining every detail of what it would be like when it finally happened to her. It was just as she'd pictured it, only a thousand times more romantic and emotional and intense than she could have ever dreamed.

A lump formed in Isabella's throat, sweeping her away with a powerful rush of love for Danny. "Thank you so much," she whispered, stroking the top of the box with a delicate fingertip.

Danny grinned slyly. "If I'd known the box would make you so happy, I wouldn't have bothered to put anything in it," he said, handing it to her. "Go ahead—open it."

Biting her lower lip, Isabella lifted the lid. Her heart nearly stopped beating at the sight of the ring. It was a square-cut white diamond with two triangular diamonds on either side, set in gold. She slipped it on her ring finger, admiring the way the gem captured the early morning sun's rays.

"It's so beautiful!" Isabella gushed breathlessly. Her glistening eyes darted from Danny to the ring and back to Danny again. "Yes! Yes, I'll marry you, Danny Wyatt!" she cried, passionately flinging her arms around his neck and pressing her lips against his.

Danny returned her kiss with decidedly less intensity, and his broad hands seemed almost hesitant as he caressed her shoulders.

Isabella pulled away from him. "Danny, what's wrong?"

A pained look creased his face. "I'm flattered that you want to marry me, Isabella, but I didn't intend for the ring to be a proposal."

"You didn't?" Isabella's voice was tight and strained. Frozen still, she stared straight at Danny, fearing that if she moved, she'd shatter into hundreds of pieces. "Then why did you give it to me?"

"I blew it. I really blew it." Danny shook his head wearily. "The ring has been in my family for generations—it belonged to my great-grandmother. There's a necklace at the bottom of the box. I thought you might want to wear it around your neck," he said, pulling out the chain. "I'm sorry I misled you. I should've given you the necklace first, I guess."

"There's no need to apologize," Isabella said quickly. An awkward smile tugged at the corners of her mouth as she slipped the ring off her finger and threaded the necklace through it. She tried to ignore the burning humiliation that seared her abdomen. "I was the one who jumped to conclusions. You didn't say anything, and I just assumed—" Her voice broke.

"You understand, don't you?" Danny asked tenderly. He put the chain around her neck and closed the clasp. "We're both so young, and there's still so much I want to do before I settle down. Marriage is such a big commitment." Danny looked deep into her eyes. "Do you understand what I'm saying?"

"Of course," Isabella answered, her smile betrayed by the tears that coursed down her cheeks. "I understand perfectly."

"What an incredible party!" Jessica Wakefield exclaimed, rubbing her tired blue-green eyes. Crossing the waiting room of the hair salon, she picked up the latest issue of *Ingenue* and took a seat by her best friend, Isabella. "I think it's going to take me weeks to recover."

One of Isabella's perfectly shaped eyebrows arched in agreement. "Me too."

Jessica played with the frayed ends of her holey jeans and smoothed out the wrinkles of her white cropped sweater. After she had gotten only two hours' sleep, it was the best outfit she could dig up on short notice. Jessica glanced admiringly at Isabella's ensemble—a funky black-and-white A-line mini, a red ribbed turtleneck, and sleek black leather knee-high boots. Even after an all-night party in her honor Isabella had no trouble pulling herself together with style.

Lifting the magazine to her mouth, Jessica stifled a yawn. "I can't believe I let you talk me into getting out of my nice, warm, cozy bed to come here for a haircut."

"A *free* haircut," Isabella corrected. "We're both so broke, we'd be crazy to turn down the offer. I only have two hundred dollars to get me through until the end of the semester."

"I wish I had *that* much. Our last shopping binge really did me in," Jessica said, her pretty pink mouth turning down into a pout. "Now I'm stuck baby-sitting Professor Wilson's kids to get a little extra cash."

Valentino, the salon's head stylist, emerged from the back room, carrying two clipboards. "It's so good to see you ladies again," he said in a vague European accent that sounded Italian one moment, French the next. The multicolored sleeves of Valentino's satin shirt billowed as he hurried toward them, but his carefully gelled hair stayed solidly in place. "You understand, of course, that this is a training session. I'm teaching my wonderful assistant Marta to cut long hair."

Jessica watched as Marta slunk past the

6

sinks and dryers to the front of the salon. She sized up Marta's black velvet cat suit and the year's supply of dark eyeliner she was wearing.

"Hello," Marta said in a throaty voice.

Jessica's heart leapt to her throat as she stared at Marta's spiky, close-cropped orange hair and the leather pouch around her waist that held five pairs of gleaming shears.

"Isn't she marvelous?" Valentino handed a clipboard to each of them. "We will be selecting the style for you today. All you have to do is sign the release form and we'll get started."

Jessica leaned toward Isabella. "There's still time," she whispered out of the corner of her mouth. "Let's make a break for it."

"Where's your sense of adventure?" Isabella signed the form with a flourish and handed the clipboard to Marta.

Valentino rubbed his chin thoughtfully. "For you, Miss Isabella, I see a nice flip, with a little layering for volume," he said in an enticing hush. "And for Miss Jessica—"

"Miss Jessica's just going to watch," Jessica interrupted, handing the unsigned form back to him. "I've changed my mind."

Isabella gave her a nudge. "Come on, Jess, it'll be fun."

Jessica sentimentally twirled a lock of her shoulder-length blond hair between her fingers. A warm beam of sunlight streaked in through the window, making it look like spun gold. She had often wondered what it would be like to have short hair, but she'd never had the courage to go through with it. And especially not now, with a nearly bald trainee who had enough chopping tools to outfit the Swiss army.

"I'm sure you'll change your mind once you see how *gorgeous* your friend looks," Valentino said with drama.

Don't bet on it, Jessica thought stubbornly. Isabella took a seat, and Marta draped a silver smock over her. Then she sprayed Isabella's hair with a water bottle. Valentino walked in ominous circles around the chair, like a vulture closing in on his prey. The tension was more than Jessica could bear.

"So what happened to the mystery guy I've heard so much about?" Isabella asked Jessica, oblivious to the flurry of activity around her. "Why didn't you bring him to the party?"

"He was busy unpacking," Jessica said evasively as she buried her head in the magazine.

Out of the corner of her eye Jessica could see that Isabella was unconvinced. "A mystery man who transferred to SVU three weeks ago," Isabella said. "You could at least tell me his name."

Jessica tossed the magazine aside. "I don't think you know him."

"Try me."

8

The corners of Jessica's mouth drooped slightly. Ever since she had met Josh Stone at an off-campus party, Jessica had avoided introducing him to her friends. It wasn't because he was a loser—in fact, he was just the opposite. Josh was tall, with a lean, athletic build, smoky blue eyes, straight white teeth, and sun-bleached blond hair that fell seductively across his face. Aside from his resemblance to a Greek god, Josh was also incredibly sweet, thoughtful, and attentive. In the three weeks Jessica had known Josh, she had been hard-pressed to find anything wrong with him.

Unfortunately Jessica's romantic past taught her that appearances could be deceiving. Behind every man she had fallen for lurked a dark demon that eventually destroyed the relationship. Sexy and dangerous Mike McAllery had swept Jessica off her feet, but their brief marriage had ended when he became abusive. James Montgomery had seemed perfect too, until Jessica had learned the hard way that he wouldn't take no for an answer. Then, of course, there was Louis Miles. He *was* perfect, and their relationship had been incredible until Louis's past had caught up with him and destroyed their love.

But Josh just seemed so—normal. *What skeletons are lurking in his closet?* she wondered. If he really did turn out to be the perfect man,

Jessica decided that she simply couldn't risk losing him.

"Maybe in a week or so I'll tell you," Jessica hedged, watching Marta comb out Isabella's long dark hair. "Right now I want to keep him all to myself."

Isabella rolled her eyes. "As if you have anything to worry about from me."

The phone rang, and Valentino headed toward the front desk. Marta finished combing through Isabella's silky hair, a sudden glimmer of inspiration lighting up her eyes. Jessica took the interruption as a perfect opportunity to change the subject.

"And how's *your* man?" Jessica asked enthusiastically. "I was going to ask you guys if you wanted to go somewhere for breakfast, but you disappeared."

"We went to the pond to watch the sunrise." The sparkle in Isabella's gray eyes suddenly went out, like a cold bucket of water being thrown on a campfire. "Danny wanted to give me my birthday gift."

Marta reached into her scissors pouch and pulled out a long sharp pair. Jessica's stomach did a double flip as Marta eyed the brand-new shears with delight.

Jessica cleared her throat nervously. "So what did you get?"

Isabella reached into her collar and pulled

out a gold necklace with a sparkling diamond ring hanging from it.

"You're *engaged?*" Jessica shouted, jumping out of her chair and rushing to Isabella's side. It surprised her that Isabella wasn't more excited with such incredible news.

"No, we're not getting married," Isabella said in a dry, almost bitter tone. "The ring belonged to Danny's great-grandmother. It's been in his family for generations."

Marta positioned the scissors just above Isabella's ear. Jessica took a close look at the ring, trying to ignore the alarming *snip, snip, snip* of Marta's scissors. It was a beautiful piece of jewelry that would make any woman envious. Obviously Danny loved Isabella very much.

"Do you guys think you'll get married someday?" Jessica asked.

Isabella's gaze was distant, her heart-shaped mouth drawing itself into a pucker. "If he asked me tomorrow, I'd say yes," she said with an odd touch of sadness in her voice. "He's definitely the person I want to spend the rest of my life with."

It must be nice to be so sure, Jessica thought grimly as she watched another silky piece of Isabella's hair tumble to the floor.

"It *is* kind of stylish . . . in its own way," Jessica said sympathetically.

11

Isabella shoved the key into the ignition of her Range Rover and buckled her seat belt. Her delicate fingers traced the uneven path of her hairline. The feeling of cool air on the back of her neck made her want to burst into tears.

"She butchered my hair!" Isabella moaned, looking at her reflection in the rearview mirror. Shaggy tufts of hair stuck out over her ears. "I can't go back to campus looking like this—the Thetas will laugh me right out of the sorority."

"Our sorority sisters aren't going to make fun of you, and if anyone says *anything,* they'll have *me* to contend with," Jessica said, rubbing Isabella's arm reassuringly. "But to tell you the truth, you're so beautiful, you can carry it off. You'd look great bald."

"Thanks, but somehow I don't find that comforting." Isabella toyed with her crooked bangs as she pulled out of the parking space. "It's going to take me years to grow my hair that length again."

"I wish there was something I could say to make you feel better." Jessica rolled down the window, letting in a burst of fresh air.

Tears burned the corners of Isabella's eyes as they traveled from the road to the rearview mirror. She watched in horror the way the wind made her hair stand on end. "I have enough problems to deal with right now—I don't need a fashion crisis to make my life even

12

worse," Isabella muttered under her breath.

Jessica clicked on the radio and cruised the airwaves. "What's wrong, Izzy? I thought things were going great for you."

"Not exactly." Isabella stared at the green traffic light in the distance, eyelashes damp with thoughts of Danny's rejection. She stepped on the gas forcefully, narrowing the gap between the Range Rover and a red Porsche several yards ahead. "Danny doesn't want to marry me."

Jessica clicked off the radio. "But I thought you said that you guys were going to get married someday," she said.

"I said I'd marry him if he asked me, but he has no intention of doing that." Isabella's voice cracked. "When Danny gave me the ring, there was a misunderstanding. I thought it was a proposal, but he made it clear that he wasn't going to get married for a long time, and even then he wasn't sure that I was the one."

"Oh, Iz—I'm so sorry." Jessica touched her lightly on the arm.

"So am I." Isabella sighed. To distract herself from the hollow, empty feeling in her chest, Isabella glanced in the mirror and tried to smooth down a stubborn cowlick.

Jessica took a pair of fashionable catlike sunglasses out of her purse and slipped them on her face. "Danny may be nervous about taking such a big step, but he loves you so much," she said. "You guys are great together. You're one of the happiest couples I've ever seen."

"I used to think so too, but I'm starting to wonder if I've been fooling myself all along." The traffic light was still green, and Isabella pressed the gas pedal as they approached the intersection. The Porsche's license plate read SURFN.

"Look at everything he did for you last night," Jessica maintained. "If that's not love, I don't know what is."

Deep down Isabella knew Jessica was right, but that didn't make it any easier. Danny had effectively put the brakes on their relationship. Did she really want to give her heart to him if they had no future together?

Isabella glared with frustration at her reflection in the mirror. "Stupid cowlick!" she hissed through bared teeth. She licked the tips of her fingers and worked furiously at the tuft of hair that stood straight up on the top of her head.

"Watch out!" Jessica shouted suddenly.

Isabella's eyes darted to the road just in time to see the red taillights of the Porsche looming only inches ahead of them.

"Oh no!" Isabella shouted. Instinctively she swerved to the right, missing the Porsche by a few inches. She stomped her foot on the brake, but the tires wouldn't grip the patch of loose gravel underneath. Isabella cut the wheel sharply as the Rover slammed into the curb with a *crunch!*

Jessica unlatched her seat belt. "I hate to say this, but that didn't sound very good."

Isabella leaned her head miserably against the steering wheel. "Please tell me things can't get any worse."

"What am I going to do?" Isabella moaned. She flung herself facedown on the old couch in the middle of her living room and buried her head in its cushions. The upholstery was an ugly brown, but Isabella had covered it with crisp green-and-white-striped linens and tied green ribbons around the legs to secure them. The couch was modern and elegant without being flashy. Just like Isabella.

"Don't worry so much." Danny's dark arms encircled Isabella's narrow waist, and he drew her closer. "I think your hair looks kind of cute," he said, running his fingers over the top of her head. "But if you feel that strongly about it, I suppose you could always buy yourself a hat."

"I'm not talking about my hair!" Isabella said with exasperation as she turned over to face him. "Hair is the least of my worries right now. I just handed over my last two hundred bucks to have the Rover towed, and who knows how much the repairs are going to be? Where am I going to get that kind of cash?"

"Why don't you call your parents and explain the situation to them?" Danny suggested.

Easier said than done, Isabella thought. Not too long ago Isabella had shared a suite on campus with Jessica. But when Jessica had moved out to get married, Isabella decided that she wanted to move into an off-campus apartment. Her parents agreed to pay the rent on the condition that her grades didn't slide. Ecstatic, Isabella found the perfect two-bedroom apartment in a building just a few yards from the edge of campus. It had a balcony with a view of Johnson Pond, and Isabella had turned the extra bedroom into a study.

"I can't ask my parents for more money," Isabella said tiredly. Her current problem temporarily overshadowed her misgivings about Danny. Without thinking twice, she pressed her cheek against Danny's muscular chest for comfort. "They're trying to build a new house and things are tight right now. A few weeks ago, when my dishwasher broke, I thought of calling. And now the cappuccino maker's on the blink too. I've got to find a way to handle it myself. I can't beg my parents to help me every time I'm in a bind."

Danny's chest rose and fell beneath her as he breathed. "Why put such a burden on yourself?

16

You know your parents would help you out."

Isabella sat up, folding her legs beneath her. "That's beside the point. I'm not a little girl anymore. I don't want to go running to Mommy and Daddy every time I get myself into a sticky situation," she said firmly. "I'll start doing manicures for people, or maybe I'll pawn a few pieces of jewelry. Whatever it takes, I'll get the money myself."

"You could always sell the ring I gave you," Danny teased.

Isabella recoiled as though she had been slapped in the face. The shock of his words stung as her fingers reached protectively for the ring. "I would never get rid of the ring, Danny! How can you even joke about it?"

Danny's face fell. "Whoa—take it easy, Isabella," he said gently. "I didn't mean to upset you. Of course I wouldn't want you to get rid of the ring. I'd be devastated."

"You would?"

"Of course I would." Danny leaned forward, his lips pressing tenderly against hers.

Isabella leaned back her head and parted her lips slightly, swept away by the passion of Danny's kiss. *Maybe I was overreacting,* she thought with relief. Danny couldn't have made it more clear that he was hopelessly in love with her.

Danny flashed her a languid smile. "I'm proud of you for deciding to take care of this yourself. I'll do anything to help you—just say the word."

"You're sweet," Isabella said happily, kissing him again.

A thoughtful expression twisted Danny's features. "Maybe I could talk to Tom—I bet he could find a job for you at the campus TV station."

Isabella bit her lower lip. "Between my course load and my activities, I don't think there's much room left for a steady job. I don't want to make a commitment to your roommate if—" Isabella suddenly stopped short.

"What is it?" Danny asked.

A slow smile broke over Isabella's face. "I think I've figured it out. I know how to get some easy cash," she said, jumping to her feet. "I'll get a roommate. We'll split the rent, and the money I save can go toward my car repairs. It's the perfect solution!"

"And you could advertise on the student bulletin board," Danny added. He grabbed a pen and a piece of paper from the table next to the couch.

Isabella walked over to the sliding glass doors that led to the balcony and stared out at the pond. A tingle of excitement moved through her like the tiny waves that rippled on the surface of the water. It was such a simple, foolproof plan, and the apartment was definitely big enough for

18

two. Her life would hardly change at all.

"Help me write the ad, Danny. I don't know how to start." She thought about it for a moment. "SVU female to share with—"

"Female," Danny quickly interjected. He jotted the ad down on the paper.

"What makes you so sure I wasn't going to say male?" Isabella teased.

Danny grinned. "Lucky guess?"

Isabella gave him a sly wink and returned to composing her ad. "I definitely need to put nonsmoker in there. I don't want any cigarette smoke stinking up the apartment."

"Nonsmoker." Danny wrote it down. "They only allow about fifteen words or so. You're already running out of space."

Isabella looked over Danny's shoulder to see what they had so far. "In large two bedroom," she dictated. "Then put call Isabella, 555-6303."

Danny handed her the finished product. "I don't know about all this, Iz," he said, a flicker of doubt in his chocolate brown eyes. "Promise me you'll be careful about choosing a roommate—you could end up with a real weirdo."

Isabella reread the ad. "Don't worry, Danny. I'll be interviewing all the candidates first," she said, happily plopping down beside him. "Besides—I'm an excellent judge of character."

Chapter Two

"So, Josh, what's your major?" Elizabeth Wakefield asked as she slid into the red vinyl booth next to her boyfriend, Tom Watts.

Here we go. Jessica stiffened. She stared across the table at her twin sister, hoping Josh was ready for the barrage of questions Elizabeth was about to hurl his way. Before they went out, Jessica had tried to prepare him. Even though they *looked* identical, Jessica and Elizabeth were completely different people.

"I was studying economics at UCLA, but I think I may switch to English." Josh took off his brown suede jacket and hung it on the chrome coatrack at the end of the booth. His smoky blue eyes were warm and receptive. "Economics seems a little too dry for my taste."

"SVU has an excellent English program,"

Tom said, running a hand through his thick brown hair.

The jukebox in the corner blared an old Elvis tune. A waitress appeared, carrying a tray of water glasses and four laminated menus.

"What do you want to do after college?" Elizabeth asked primly. Her long blond braid and conservative cotton blouse made her seem years older than Jessica, even though in reality they had been born only four minutes apart.

Jessica nervously snatched a menu from the stack and buried her face in it, perspiration beading along the scoop neck of her black form-fitting baby T-shirt. *She's worse than Mom and Dad,* Jessica thought miserably. Jessica knew that since Elizabeth was an investigative reporter, she thought it was her duty to interview all Jessica's prospective boyfriends. At the end of the night Jessica could look forward to a full report, whether she wanted it or not.

"I haven't exactly decided on a career yet," Josh answered, taking a sip from his water glass. "I'm toying with the idea of teaching or maybe trying my hand at journalism."

Jessica peeked over the top of the menu, catching the look of subtle approval on Elizabeth's face. Even straightlaced Tom brightened a little.

"Elizabeth and I run WSVU—the campus television station," Tom said breezily. "We're always looking for new blood. If you want to give reporting a shot, we'd love to have you on board."

Jessica dropped the menu on the tabletop and looked at Josh. In the past Jessica's boyfriends were usually squirming at this point in the interview, but Josh just leaned back easily, putting his strong arm around her shoulders.

"That sounds great," he said with a relaxed smile that made Jessica weak in the knees. He turned toward Jessica, blond bangs falling across his forehead, and winked. "I just might take you up on that offer."

Elizabeth nodded encouragingly. "I hope you will."

Jessica exhaled, the knots in her neck slowly unraveling. "Is everyone ready to order?" she asked, clapping. "I'm starved."

"What a great living room!" A woman with long red hair and a nose ring surveyed Isabella's apartment with the scrutinizing eye of an interior decorator. She was the first in a long line of candidates who had responded to the ad Isabella had posted in the student union. "There's just enough room in the corner for my drum set."

One of Isabella's perfectly shaped eyebrows rose a fraction of an inch. "You play drums?"

The woman looked down modestly, as if she had been given a compliment. "Well, yeah, but I promise I won't get in your way," she said. "I only practice two hours a day—from six in the morning until eight."

Not here, you won't, Isabella thought ruefully.

The second candidate, a freshman named Anita, showed up with her parents. Anita hardly said a word, but her parents grilled Isabella as if they were cross-examining her in a courtroom.

"Anita likes to eat around six o'clock and should be in bed no later than eleven," Anita's mom said, patting her daughter proudly on the arm. She handed Isabella a packet of papers. "Here are the dates of all her exams this semester. Make sure she starts studying at least two weeks in advance."

Isabella smiled meekly, but inside she wanted to scream, *What do I look like? A baby-sitter?* Once the parents were out of earshot, Anita leaned over and whispered to Isabella. "Do me a favor and tell them you'll let me move in just to get them off my case. They don't know it, but I'm moving in with my boyfriend, Spike, next week."

Appointment numbers three and four never showed up.

Candidate number five had already hired a

moving van. When Isabella opened the door, she was bombarded with boxes and furniture piled in the hallway. "Hi—I'm Chandra," the candidate said boldly, holding out her hand. "I'm your new roommate."

While Isabella spent the next hour trying to convince Chandra that she wasn't allowed to move in, several candidates came and went, mistakenly thinking that Isabella had already found a new roommate.

"Are you sure you don't want me to stay? My stuff is already here," Chandra pleaded as the moving men returned to the truck.

Isabella gritted her teeth. "Thanks for stopping by," she said, practically pushing Chandra out into the hall. The phone rang. "Good luck finding a place to live," Isabella shouted through the door.

Isabella grabbed the phone off the cradle. "Hello?" she breathed into the receiver. It was the mechanic at the garage, calling with the repair estimate. The damage to the Range Rover came to two thousand dollars.

"Are you sure?" Isabella gripped the edge of the telephone stand to steady herself. She had known it was going to be an expensive repair, but she never dreamed it would be that high.

"Major work needs to be done," the mechanic said. "The axle's bent, plus you need an alignment and new front tires, and one of your rims is dented. Do you want us to go ahead with the work?"

Isabella rubbed the tense muscles in her shoulder. "I don't know yet. I have to think about it."

"You can't let it sit here. It's taking up space," the mechanic said. "If you want, we can tow it somewhere else."

"No," Isabella said urgently, gripping the receiver with white knuckles. "I just need a little time. Can you give me a day?"

"All right." The mechanic sighed. "Call me tomorrow before closing time."

Isabella hung up the phone and slumped into a kitchen chair. She still didn't have a roommate, and the search was a complete disaster. Isabella had been so sure her plan would work, she hadn't even thought of a backup. Time was closing in on her, and the bills kept piling up. Hot tears of desperation sprang to her eyes. "What am I going to do?"

"I love Josh," Elizabeth said, squeezing the soap dispenser and working her hands into a lather. "He seems like a great guy."

Jessica stared at her sister's reflection in the mirror, arms folded across her bare midriff. They were in the bathroom at the restaurant. Tom and Josh were waiting for them back at their table. "If *you* approve of him, something must be wrong. I'd better break up with him."

"Don't you *dare*." Elizabeth turned on the hand dryer. "Hold on to Josh—this guy is a gem."

Jessica opened her patent-leather makeup bag and took out a lip-liner pencil. Carefully she traced just beyond the outline of her lips to make them appear fuller, then filled in the color with a matching lipstick. "He does seem like a great guy, Liz, but I've been through this before. Every guy I've ever been with has turned out to be trouble, so why should Josh be any different?"

"You're not being fair," Elizabeth said, pulling a few soft wisps of hair around her beautiful face. "Josh hasn't done anything to deserve your mistrust. Maybe he really is as perfect as he seems."

A painful lump formed in Jessica's throat. "The last thing I need is a perfect guy. I thought Louis was perfect—and look what happened to him."

Elizabeth placed a comforting hand on Jessica's arm. "Don't do that to yourself, Jessica," she said. "Every time we fall in love, we risk being hurt. But that's part of what makes love so precious. Imagine if you'd never met Louis."

"I wouldn't have had to go through the

torture of losing him," Jessica answered thickly, zipping up her makeup bag.

"But you also would've missed out on the incredible experiences you had together," Elizabeth countered.

Jessica glared at her red-rimmed eyes in the mirror. Grieving over Louis's death was like opening a vein—draining all the lifeblood out of her. It left her timid and afraid. For Jessica there was no love without heartbreak.

"Besides," Elizabeth added, "Louis's situation was pretty unique. I doubt you'll find an insane ex-wife lingering in Josh's past."

Jessica smiled reluctantly. "You're probably right," she said, brushing the hair out of her face and tucking it behind her ear. She reached out and gave her twin sister a hug. "Thanks, Liz."

Elizabeth hugged her back, then checked her watch. "We've been in here for a while. The guys will probably think we took off without them."

Jessica grabbed her bag and headed for the door, suddenly stopping short. "Just one thing," she said, hand poised on the door handle. "Do you think Josh is cute?"

"He's a total babe." Elizabeth sighed, rolling her eyes for emphasis. Her lips curled into a slight smirk. "But don't tell Tom I said that."

*   *   *

"Hello? Is anyone home?"

Startled, Isabella lifted her head off the kitchen table, her face hot and puffy from crying. A mousy young woman with long, stringy hair stood awkwardly in the doorway. Her shoulders slouched forward, puckering the front of her wrinkled, baggy brown dress.

"I didn't mean to frighten you," the mousy woman said apologetically, her voice low and unsure. "But the door was open."

Isabella quickly wiped away a stray tear and blew her nose on a paper napkin. "Do I know you?"

The woman leaned against the doorway. "I called about the apartment. My name is Lisa Fontaine." She tucked a stringy strand of hair behind her ear and shifted her weight from one foot to the other. "If this is a bad time, I could come back."

An embarrassed laugh escaped Isabella's lips. She cleared her throat and ran a swift finger under each eye to remove all traces of runny mascara. "Now is as bad a time as any."

Lisa closed the door and shuffled toward the kitchen set. "You don't look so hot."

"I've definitely been better," Isabella answered.

Chewing nervously on her fingernails, Lisa seemed to study Isabella for a moment with her dull hazel eyes. "Do you want me to make you some coffee or something?"

Isabella's talent for sparkling conversation escaped her temporarily as she struggled to gain her composure. "Actually that would be very nice," she said gratefully.

Without saying another word, Lisa filled the cappuccino maker with water. She turned the nozzle to make steam, but a violent spray of water came spurting out like a lawn sprinkler. "How do you turn it off?" Lisa squealed.

Using one arm to shield her eyes, Isabella found the nozzle and turned it off. "I forgot to mention that the cappuccino maker is broken," Isabella said as they both slid in the puddle of water on the floor. Completely drenched, Isabella and Lisa broke into fits of laughter. "I'm really sorry."

"It's all right," Lisa said, reaching for a dry kitchen towel. Isabella noticed that when she smiled, Lisa actually looked quite pretty. "It would be pretty simple to fix, you know. I could take a look at it if you want."

"You know how to fix my cappuccino maker?"

Lisa's head fell slightly, wet ropes of hair dropping into her eyes. "People have told me I'm handy," she said modestly.

Grabbing a sponge mop out of the closet, Isabella wiped up the wet floor. *It would be nice*

29

to have a roommate who knows her way around a set of tools, she thought. "What year are you, Lisa?"

Lisa cleaned the counter with a few paper towels. "Sophomore—but I'm a transfer student."

"Oh?" Isabella ran her long fingers through her damp hair. "Where did you transfer from?"

"New York University," Lisa answered. "I grew up in Manhattan."

Isabella smiled. "I love New York, especially in the fall. There's such a feeling of expectation in the air. Did you ever go to those little art shows they have on the sidewalk near Washington Square Park?"

"Every year for as long as I can remember," Lisa said, wiping her forehead with the sleeve of her brown dress.

Wringing out the mop in the sink, Isabella paused for a moment, her stunning gray eyes lost in thought. "I have a friend from high school who goes to NYU," she mused. "Maybe you know her. Her name is Carolyn Baxter."

Lisa set the sponge on the counter, letting her arms dangle limply at her sides. "No, the name doesn't sound familiar."

Isabella leaned against the mop handle. "I can't quite remember which NYU building she lives in—is there one by Union Square? I forget."

"Probably," Lisa answered. "There are a lot of different dorms."

"It doesn't matter," Isabella said, snapping out of her reverie. "But it would've been interesting if you two had run into each other at some point."

Lisa nodded and continued to clean up.

Isabella's body began to relax. It was amazing how at ease she felt around Lisa. Even though she wasn't the type of girl Isabella usually hung out with, Isabella found herself chatting endlessly in her presence. Lisa was neat, handy, and quiet, and they seemed to have hit it off instantly. *I've got a good feeling about this one,* Isabella thought. She could feel it deep down in her gut.

"So when do you think you could move in?" Isabella said, putting the kettle on for tea.

Lisa's eyes widened with surprise. "You really want me to move in?"

"Why not?" Isabella answered. "Do you want to move in?"

"Sure—I could do it anytime," Lisa said eagerly. Then suddenly her face fell. "All my references are in New York. It might be kind of hard getting in touch with them."

"Never mind about that," Isabella said confidently, pulling two mugs down from the cupboard. "I know a good roommate when I see one."

*　　*　　*

"Are you sure this is everything?" Isabella asked, looking at the worn duffel bag and small cardboard box that Lisa had brought.

Unlike the last time Lisa had seen her, Isabella was fresh faced and composed. Her hair was coaxed into a chic style with a bit of gel, and she wore a copper-colored tunic over a pair of ribbed leggings.

"Most of my stuff is still in storage in New York," Lisa explained, her face burning with embarrassment because she was wearing the same brown dress that she'd worn the day before. She picked up the bag and box and followed Isabella to the bedroom. "I'm still waiting for my old roommate to ship it. We had a fight before I left, so I'm not even sure if she's going to send my stuff to me."

Isabella turned on her heel, her perfect features taking on a curious expression. Even walking through her apartment with no one around, Isabella moved with the grace of an international fashion model strutting down the runways of Europe. "If you don't mind me asking, what did you guys fight about?"

How could you be so stupid? Lisa wanted to kick herself. It had to be a complete fluke that Isabella decided to choose her as a roommate, and the last thing Lisa needed was to give her a reason to change her mind. "It was nothing, really," Lisa said quickly, comparing Isabella's delicate leather heels to her own clumsy, mud-covered hiking boots. "She borrowed some money from me and refused to pay it back."

Isabella nodded knowingly. "I've seen many friendships wrecked over money. I hope you can get your stuff back."

"Yeah, me too," Lisa said, trying to untangle a knot of hair that had formed at the nape of her neck.

Isabella flicked on the light switch, revealing a small, rectangular room with plain white walls and a folded futon in the corner. A wooden desk was pushed underneath the only window. There were no curtains, and the shade was drawn. "That's the bathroom," Isabella said, pointing to the door next to the closet. "It joins this room with my bedroom. I'm sorry it's so bare in here—I was using it as a study and guest room for when my friends wanted to crash. The futon's comfortable, but we can get you a real bed if you want it."

Lisa put down the bag, scanning every corner of the room with wide-eyed fascination. "I think it's nice," she said softly.

"Good." Isabella laughed with relief. Her laughter filled the room like the sound of hundreds of tiny silver bells. "I'll help you unpack, then I'll give you a tour of the whole building."

Lisa hid behind her curtain of stringy hair, not wanting Isabella to catch a full view of her face. She was ashamed of her high forehead, wide-set eyes, and thin lips. There was no doubt in Lisa's mind that someone like Isabella, with her sculpted cheekbones and milky smooth skin, would be revolted at the sight of her.

"So what do you think of SVU so far?" Isabella asked, unpacking the cardboard box.

Lisa unzipped the duffel bag and pulled out two dresses, identical to the one she was wearing, and a long brown coat. "Oh, I like it a lot," she said shyly. "There are a lot of cute guys."

"I know what you mean." Isabella smiled.

Lisa hung up her clothes. The three modest pieces looked lost in the huge, empty closet. She turned around, and with a sudden burst of courage she said, "Are you popular?"

Isabella blinked at Lisa for a moment, as if she didn't quite know how to respond. Lisa waited patiently, dying to know the answer.

"I have quite a few friends, if that's what you mean," Isabella said slowly.

Lisa nodded appreciatively. "I thought you would. You seem like that kind of person."

With an awkward smile Isabella emptied the cardboard container. "What a gorgeous rosewood box," she said, pulling out a small wooden box with a rose carved into the lid. She held it up and looked at it from all sides. "Where did you get it?"

Lisa's shy smile faded, as if a dark cloud had descended upon her. She stomped over to where Isabella was standing. "It's none of your business!" Lisa shrilled, yanking the box out of Isabella's hands.

Chapter
Three

"Would the lady care for another slice of apple?" Josh asked, reaching into the wicker picnic basket he had brought. The bright California sun's rays heightened the stunning contrast between his white blond hair and the bronze color of his tanned skin.

Jessica had insisted they meet at the public park in the center of town, since she still wasn't quite ready to share Josh with the rest of the SVU population. She knew she couldn't keep him to herself forever, especially now that Josh's classes were starting. Soon girls would be to swarming him from all directions, but at least she'd managed to get a good head start.

Jessica stretched out on the lawn, feeling the velvety green grass press against the bare back of her denim halter. She imagined herself the sovereign queen of some tiny but fashionable aristocracy, where she'd be waited on hand and foot by gorgeous, muscular servants. "Yes—the lady *would* like another slice of apple," she said in a noble tone. "And put some of that Brie stuff on it too."

"As you wish," Josh said, kissing the tip of her nose.

Jessica sighed contentedly, watching the clouds roll by from behind her sunglasses. She was glad she had taken her sister's advice to give Josh the benefit of the doubt. So far everything he had done was flawless. Josh seemed to know Jessica's likes and dislikes without even asking.

Josh handed Jessica the apple slice, licking a bit of juice off his fingertips. "I had fun with Elizabeth and Tom last night. We should do it again sometime."

"Next time I'll have to bring a pillow. Every time Liz and Tom start talking about WSVU, I have this uncontrollable urge to nod off to sleep," Jessica said, savoring the flavors of the crisp, tart apple and the rich, creamy cheese melding in her mouth. "Whenever those two are together, it's a total snorefest."

"I don't think they're *that* bad." Josh reclined on the grass, propping his head up with one hand. "They're just serious, that's all. Actually I'm kind of excited about the work they're doing at WSVU. Once I get settled in with my classes, I think I might take Tom up on his offer."

Jessica's eyes bulged. "You were serious about working at WSVU?"

"Why wouldn't I be? It's a good chance for me to find out if I'm cut out for journalism."

"I thought you were humoring them—just making conversation," Jessica said.

Josh shook his head. "One thing you should learn about me, Jessica, is that I never say anything I don't really mean."

Finishing the last bit of apple, Jessica turned her head toward Josh, feeling the gentle prickle of grass against her cheek. *Are you for real?* she wondered, studying his neutral expression. Were Josh's smoky eyes serious or laughing at her from behind his dark sunglasses? Since there was no reason not to believe him, trust was the only other option.

The heat of the noonday sun made Jessica's shoulders tingle with the impending threat of sunburn. She reached into her canvas backpack for a tube of sunblock. "We could be at the beach right now if I didn't have a stupid geology exam in two hours," she said with a groan.

Josh took a long drink from his plastic water bottle. "As soon as we both have some free time, we'll go to the beach. My friend has a beach house in Malibu. He said he'd let me borrow it some weekend when he's out of town."

"You're kidding!" Jessica squealed with delight. "We *have* to go to Malibu, Josh—it would be so incredible!"

Josh's mouth curved into a smile. "I promise—we will."

Jessica sighed to herself as she rubbed the sunblock onto her arms. So far Josh was scoring points on all fronts, but the biggest test of all was yet to come. A few yards away, on the paved walking path, Jessica spotted an in-line skating beauty sporting a dangerous red bikini that was distracting enough to cause a train wreck. The young woman skated across the park, leaving a trail of devastated Frisbee players in her wake.

"Look at that," Jessica said with mock outrage, noting Josh's reaction out of the corner of her eye. "Some people have absolutely no *decency.*"

Josh looked up at the Roller Derby queen, his jaw practically dropping to his knees.

I knew it, Jessica thought with annoyance. *He's an animal, just like every other male on this campus.* She shot him a look. "Come on, Josh, at least have the courtesy not to drool in front of me."

"I'm sorry," Josh muttered, slowly sliding his shades down to the tip of his nose. To Jessica's shock, Josh's eyes weren't focused on the woman's well-endowed body but instead were glued to her feet. "Those are the coolest blades I've ever seen," he said as she rolled by, his eyes never moving higher than her ankle. "I've been shopping for some new skates. Are you into blading?"

"Sure," Jessica said, still stunned.

"Great," Josh answered as he reached for the sunblock and started massaging it into Jessica's shoulders. "Maybe we can blade when we get to Malibu."

What did I do wrong? Isabella set aside the small wooden box, avoiding Lisa's fierce gaze. "I didn't mean to pry," she apologized quickly. "Maybe we should just forget about unpacking for a while. Let me show you around the building instead."

Lisa followed silently as Isabella led her out of the apartment and down the hallway to the stairwell. Isabella's body tensed, waiting for Lisa to say something—anything—but she remained silent. The sudden change in Lisa's mood electrified the air, like an impending thunderstorm.

"Normally we could take the elevator, but it's not working right now. To tell you the truth, it's always breaking down," Isabella explained, very aware of the forced lightness in her voice. She gave Lisa a quick sideways glance. Lisa still didn't respond. "The thought of getting stuck in an elevator scares me so much, I usually take the stairs," Isabella chatted aimlessly. "Plus climbing five flights is a great workout."

The exit door to the fifth floor slammed shut behind them, the clean, metallic sound echoing down the stairwell. Isabella took the stairs carefully, making sure not to trip in her slippery stack-heeled shoes. Lisa trailed behind, her hiking boots clopping heavily like the hooves of an untrained horse.

Isabella stopped at the third-floor landing and turned around. Lisa's silence was unbearable.

"If we're going to be roommates, I think it's important for us to be open and honest with each other," Isabella started.

Lisa looked down. Glimpses of her pasty complexion and hollow cheeks appeared in between tangled ropes of brown hair. Her pointed toe traced invisible arcs on the tiled floor.

"I'm sorry I touched your things," Isabella continued. "I didn't mean any harm."

Lisa's foot stopped moving. Raising her eyes, she pushed her stringy bangs out of her face.

Isabella smiled, grateful to finally have eye contact but slightly disturbed by Lisa's extreme shyness. Lisa was like a timid caterpillar, trapped safely in her own little cocoon. What would it take to get her out of her shell?

"Since we're living together, I was kind of hoping we could be friends," Isabella said.

Confusion flickered in Lisa's dull eyes. "*You* want to be friends with *me?*" Lisa pointed to herself.

"Why not? You seem like a perfectly nice person." Isabella continued down the stairs while Lisa followed in tow. "But if you don't want to be friends with me, I'll understand."

"Of course I do!" Lisa gushed with a sudden rush of emotion. "I'm just surprised, that's all."

"Well, don't be," Isabella said with a smile.

When they reached the basement, Isabella tugged on the drab gray door, and it creaked open, revealing a dark, damp cavern on the other side. A pungent wave of mildew assaulted them and faint liquid sounds dripped in the distance. The furnace hummed.

"I hate it down here—it's totally creepy," Isabella said, crouching into the dark hallway. Even though the basement ceiling was at least two feet taller than she was, Isabella kept her head low for fear of brushing against a dangling spiderweb. She felt for the light switch and clicked it on, illuminating an exposed lightbulb at the end of the hall. "I try to come down here as little as possible.

42

When your stuff arrives from New York, you can keep the boxes in one of the storage areas."

The hallway snaked in a sort of squared S shape. As they turned the first corner darkness fell again until Isabella located the next switch. To their left, the locked wire storage cages seemed to rise and shift with the moving shadows. Suddenly something inside one of the cages fell with a *thud*.

"What was that?" Isabella said, panicking.

Lisa was hardly startled at all. "Maybe it was a rat."

Isabella's heart pounded with sickening dread. They took another hard left and her paced quickened, hands urgently finding each light switch by memory. The musty air clung to Isabella's hair and clothes. At the end of the long hall they turned right. "Even though it's a major hassle, I wash my clothes at the coin laundry in town," she said, pointing out the dank laundry room. "It's better than coming down here."

"What's that?" Lisa pointed to a door with chipping paint and a rusted door handle.

"It's the tool closet," Isabella answered. "You can borrow anything you want in there."

Lisa opened the door. "Cool," she said, looking at the shelves loaded with old screwdrivers, a few hammers, a drill set, and glass jars filled with rusted nails. "I can use some of this stuff to fix the cappuccino maker."

The furnace grew louder, making the thin metal air-conditioning ducts that were suspended from the ceiling rattle. They had finally reached the last stretch of hallway, with the old-fashioned elevator in the middle and the furnace at the dead end. "Over here is the incinerator," Isabella said, pointing to a big metal box with a circular door in the middle. A pungent, foul odor suddenly hit them. Isabella covered her nose and mouth. Her stomach heaved.

"It looks like someone left their garbage out," Lisa said flatly.

A big bag of garbage was lying on its side in the corner. For some reason people were always leaving their garbage by the incinerator instead of throwing it in and burning it like they were supposed to. The bag was torn open, its contents strewn all over the floor. A sleek black body and a long thin tail crawled around in the filth.

"There's a rat!" Isabella screamed, tugging at Lisa's sleeve. "Let's get out of here!"

Lisa didn't move. She watched, a look of fascination lighting her eyes. "He's kind of cute." She giggled.

"Oh yeah, *real* cute." Isabella grimaced in disgust. "Come on, Lisa, let's go."

As if she didn't hear her, Lisa crouched

down and picked up a crust of bread off the floor. She held it out and made a clucking sound with her tongue, trying to feed the rat by hand. "I could keep him in my room—in a cage, of course," she said, coaxing the rat to come nearer. The rodent's beady black eyes surveyed Lisa for a moment before it returned to the pile of trash. "We could give him a name."

Isabella's lunch churned restlessly in her stomach. "Don't go near him, Lisa. He'll bite you. He's probably rabid."

"He's just a harmless little creature," Lisa said, pouting her lips as if she were talking to a newborn. She dropped the crust of bread in front of the rat. "You're just a harmless little guy, aren't you, fella?"

"How's it working out with your new roommate?" Jessica asked Isabella the following afternoon as they lounged in the elegant parlor of the Theta sorority house. The weekly Theta meeting had just ended, and the sisters were mingling, nibbling on miniature pastries, and catching up on all the latest campus news.

"I'm not quite sure yet," Isabella said in a confidential tone. The antique filigree earrings that dangled from her earlobes captured the soft glow of a stained glass table lamp nearby.

She smoothed the front of her straight silk skirt and gracefully crossed her legs. "Lisa seems a little . . . odd."

Jessica leaned in closer, delighted at the prospect of a juicy piece of gossip. "Like how?"

"She's always hiding behind her long, stringy hair and baggy clothes," Isabella said as tactfully as possible. "I know there's a beautiful girl somewhere in there just dying to come out."

"I spy a makeover candidate," Jessica said. "It sounds like a great weekend project."

Isabella nodded, pursing her lips thoughtfully. "But then I was thinking, why should I care about how she dresses?"

"As far as I'm concerned, looking great is a public service," Jessica said, admiring her own carefully orchestrated ensemble in the oval wall mirror. She wore men's tailored pinstriped pants and suspenders over a very clingy, very feminine blouse. "I mean, why pollute the world with bad fashion?"

Isabella threw back her head and laughed. "Seriously, Jess, there's more to it than that. Lisa's incredibly shy and quiet—she's the most introverted person I've ever met." She paused, gray eyes darting around the room, as if she were afraid someone might overhear. Her voice was just above a whisper. "Yesterday when I was showing her the basement of our apartment building, we saw a huge rat near the incinerator. Lisa wasn't even scared—if you can believe it. In fact, she wanted to keep the horrible thing as a pet. Isn't that strange?"

Jessica's nose turned up slightly. "That *is* pretty nasty," she had to admit. "But maybe Lisa's just one of those people who love all living things—no matter how disgusting they might be."

Isabella rubbed her forehead with her perfectly manicured fingertips. "I'm probably just being mean. I've hardly known her long enough to make an accurate judgment. After all, she did seem kind of nice when we first met."

"Lisa could be Godzilla and it wouldn't matter." Jessica tossed her golden mane of hair over one shoulder. "The fact is, you need the money. She has to stick around at least until your car is paid for."

Magda Helperin, the sorority president, strolled by the couch with a glass of lemonade in hand, smiling at them both. "I love your new haircut, Isabella."

"Thanks." Isabella touched the back of her head and laughed. "Did Jess tell you the whole sordid story?"

Magda nodded. "But I must say that it doesn't look nearly as bad as I imagined. In fact, it's quite flattering."

"Izzy can pull off *anything*," Jessica said proudly.

A pinkish glow colored Isabella's milky cheeks. "I went to the drugstore and bought nearly every hair product they had, hoping to salvage it."

"You really do look great," Denise Waters added, her curls bouncing as she plopped down on the end of the couch. "How much do you want to bet that by the end of the week every girl on this campus will have short hair just like Isabella's?"

A group of Thetas started cheering and clapping.

"Thanks for the vote of confidence, ladies," Isabella said with a smile. "But enough about my hair. What I want to know is if any of you know who Jessica's new boyfriend is."

The Thetas gathered around, grilling each other for information. Jessica grinned with the satisfaction of knowing that they didn't have a clue.

"Come on, Jess," Denise pleaded. "We're your sisters—you have to tell us."

Isabella's face held a look of intense curiosity. "Who is he?"

Jessica paused, enjoying the drama of the moment. "Why is my boyfriend's identity so intriguing to all of you?"

"Because you always tell us everything

about your boyfriends," Denise explained.

"Even more than we want to know," Magda added dryly.

Jessica grinned coyly. "This time I thought I'd take a different approach. I didn't want to say anything until I was sure we'd be together for a while. No false alarms."

"So are you sure yet?" Sonya Wilson asked, her green eyes wide with interest.

Isabella glared impatiently at Jessica. "When are we going to meet him?"

Savoring the attention coming at her from all sides, Jessica leaned back against the cushions contentedly. "Soon enough, ladies," she said with a sigh. "You'll all meet him soon enough."

"Coffee's ready!" Isabella called from the kitchen.

Lisa finished tightening the leaky bathroom faucet with a wrench she had found in the basement. "I'll be there in a minute!"

I can't believe I'm living here, Lisa thought with pure delight. The apartment was by far the nicest she'd ever seen, and Isabella was probably the nicest person she'd ever met. But it was too good to last. Lisa felt as if she were living some incredible dream, knowing full well that one day she'd have to wake up.

Lisa put the wrench back into the toolbox and washed her hands with one of the little pink soaps Isabella had arranged in a basket on the edge of the sink. She dried her hands on an embroidered hand towel, her eyes taking in the tastefully decorated bathroom. From the dried wreath of flowers on the door to the carefully stenciled ivy pattern on the walls to the scented candle floating in a glass bowl—everything was perfect.

Except me, Lisa thought as she stared at her reflection in the mirror. Her complexion was sallow, her eyes sunken. The drabness of her hair and dress contrasted painfully with the decor. *Why did Isabella pick me to live with her?* Lisa felt like a walking garbage heap spreading ugliness wherever she went. She had been too lucky to land a place like this—it was only a matter of time before Isabella realized it too.

"Are you coming?" Isabella called a second time. "Everything's ready."

Lisa tried to brush out the creases and wrinkles of her dress, although it didn't do much good, and went into the kitchen. The rich scent of coffee welcomed her.

"The sink's all fixed," Lisa announced, taking a seat at the kitchen table. Isabella had put out two dainty white coffee cups with saucers and a basket of chocolate chip cookies. They looked delicious. "After coffee I'll get started on the dishwasher."

Isabella stirred a spoonful of sugar into her

cup. The edges of her lips turned down slightly. "Please, Lisa, you just got here—relax."

A pang of embarrassment twinged inside Lisa. She was only trying to be helpful. She only wanted Isabella to like her. *You overdid it,* Lisa scolded herself. *You overdid it and now Isabella hates you.*

"You don't like what I've done?" Lisa's voice wavered, and worry lines creased her forehead.

"Of course I do," Isabella said reassuringly, her delicate hand lightly touching her long, slender throat. "I like it a lot. But you don't have to fix everything in one day. After all, you're my roommate, not a hired hand."

My roommate. There was a magical sound to it—a comforting ring that resounded pleasantly in Lisa's mind. There was a connection between her and Isabella. She belonged to Isabella. She was Isabella's *roommate.*

The tension in Lisa's face gave way as she giggled out loud. "I like living here."

Isabella's crimson lips parted in a wide smile. Lisa noticed that the color of her lipstick was the exact same shade as her long, glossy nails. Isabella's perfectly manicured hands were a far cry from Lisa's own bitten, peeling nails. "I'm glad you're here," she said, gracefully handing Lisa the basket. "Would you like a cookie?"

Lisa's mouth watered as she reached into

the basket. Her hands moved from cookie to cookie, trying to find the softest ones. She grabbed four and hungrily popped a whole one into her mouth. They were still warm.

"It's the first time I've used this recipe." Isabella took only one cookie for herself. "I hope they're OK."

Nodding, Lisa devoured another cookie in one bite. "They're the best I've ever had," she said with a full mouth. Lisa looked up to see Isabella eating with precise little nibbles, stopping in between bites to take sips of coffee. Lisa stopped chewing, feeling like a complete slob next to someone so cultured, so refined. In shame she covered her mouth with a napkin as the remainder of the warm chocolate cookie oozed down her throat.

"I have an idea—tell me what you think." Isabella's silver bangles jingled musically as she set down her coffee cup. "Since your clothes haven't arrived yet from New York, I thought maybe we could go shopping tomorrow. It'll be a chance for us to get to know each other a little better."

Lisa's hazel eyes bulged. "I haven't been shopping in years." She surveyed Isabella's black crushed velvet bodysuit and expensive-looking designer jeans. Even in casual clothes Isabella looked totally polished. "I wouldn't know what to get."

"Then you're in luck," Isabella with triumph. "Because *I'm* an expert shopper. In fact, if shopping were an Olympic event, I'd win the gold. I'll help you pick out something fabulous."

Lisa was about to sink her teeth into another cookie when she stopped herself, choosing to nibble on it instead. "Would you?" she asked, her heart beating faster. "Do you think you could help me pick out a whole new outfit?"

"I know some great stores that aren't too expensive. By the end of the day we'll have you looking like a fashion model."

"I can't wait!" Lisa's mind raced as she imagined all the beautiful clothes she could buy. *Isabella does like me after all, and we're going shopping together tomorrow.* It was too much to take in all at once. Lisa knew she would be too excited to sleep that night.

Isabella held her coffee cup high in the air, pinky finger extended like royalty, and proposed a toast. "To roommates," she said.

Lisa lifted her own cup happily, her fingers fumbling as she tried to imitate Isabella's graceful style. She clinked the cups together and smiled. "To roommates."

Chapter Four

"There's so much to choose from, I don't know where to start!" Lisa exclaimed, bounding from one clothing rack to the next. "This place is incredible!"

Isabella stood off to the side of the store by the wall mirror, watching Lisa's childlike eyes soak up the atmosphere. It was an average clothing store that could be found in any mall across America and was certainly nothing compared to the Fifth Avenue stores that Lisa must have seen in New York. But for some reason Lisa couldn't seem to get enough. Her jaw went slack and her hazel eyes actually sparkled, as though she had just discovered a secret room brimming with priceless jewels.

"Look at this!" Lisa shouted, pulling a dress off the closest rack. The cut was nearly identical to the baggy dress she was already wearing, but the material was a blue-and-green plaid with a lace collar. Lisa held the dress lovingly against her body, looking at her reflection in the mirror. "What do you think?"

"It's nice," Isabella said, carefully disguising her horror. "But I had something else in mind." With an expert eye she scanned a nearby rack and found a double-breasted black blazer with silver buttons and a matching slim skirt. "How about this? You can wear the pieces together or separately, so it's like getting three new outfits."

Lisa frowned. "I don't think so," she said, shaking her head. "*You* would look great in it, but I'd look stupid."

"No, you wouldn't!" Isabella held the hanger in front of Lisa.

"Yes, I would," Lisa said, pushing it away. She grabbed Isabella's hand and pulled her in front of the long mirror. "Look how gorgeous you are and look how frumpy *I* am."

The contrast between them was obvious, and if Isabella had tried to deny it, she'd look like a liar. But Lisa *was* pretty underneath her rough exterior. Isabella sensed that given the opportunity, Lisa would blossom.

"You're not so frumpy, Lisa. You have great cheekbones for one, and a beautiful smile," she said truthfully. "If you really want to make a change in your appearance, all you need is a little makeup, maybe a haircut, and more flat-tering clothes. You'll look great, I promise."

Squinting, Lisa stared hard at the mirror. "I just don't see it."

"Try on the suit," Isabella coaxed. "It's a start."

After hesitating for a moment or two, Lisa took the hanger and disappeared into the changing room.

"You won't regret it," Isabella called after her. While she waited for Lisa to change, Isabella searched the blouse racks for some-thing colorful to complement Lisa's complex-ion. *I can't wait to see how she looks*, Isabella thought excitedly. She had never met anyone so lacking in self-confidence, and Isabella couldn't help wondering what had happened to Lisa to make her feel that way. Did someone hurt her in the past?

Nevertheless, Isabella was grateful to have such a quiet, clean, considerate roommate. Even though Lisa could be terribly naive, it was kind of fun introducing her to new things. Lisa was like the little sister Isabella never had.

"I don't know if I should come out," Lisa said doubtfully, poking her head out of the dressing room.

Isabella waved at her to come out. "Stand in the three-way mirror so I can get a good look."

Slowly Lisa stepped out. She bumbled over to the mirror, eyes glued to the floor and hair draped across her face.

"Stand up straight and lift your chin," Isabella directed gently as she smoothed down the lapels of the blazer.

Lisa looked up and pulled back her shoulders. The suit was a perfect fit, following the curves of her trim waist and womanly hips. The skirt stopped just above the knee, showing off a great pair of legs. Apparently Lisa's baggy dresses had been hiding a terrific figure.

"How do I look?" she asked nervously.

Isabella ran her fingers through Lisa's thin hair, moving it out of her eyes and rolling it into a loose French twist. She turned Lisa around so that she faced the mirror. "What do *you* think?"

Lisa studied her reflection for a long time. She turned from side to side, sometimes looking with serious fascination, other times the corners of her mouth turning up in a hesitant smile.

"Who is that?" Lisa said to the mirror.

Isabella smiled warmly. "A beautiful woman."

They spent the entire afternoon shopping, and by the time they left the store, Lisa had a bought the suit, a pair of jeans, two blouses, a sweater, a pair of black pumps, a lariat necklace, and a matching pair of earrings.

"I'd say this shopping trip was a complete success." Isabella stood on the edge of the curb and flagged down a cab.

Lisa stuffed the shopping bags into the backseat of the cab and squeezed in next to Isabella. "But you didn't buy anything," she said.

"I'm too broke." Isabella was suddenly reminded that her car was supposed to be ready in two days. It was going to be nice not to have to take a cab whenever she wanted to leave campus. "It was fun watching you, though. You've got a whole new wardrobe."

Lisa smiled broadly. A tinge of color came to her normally pale skin. "Thanks for everything, Isabella. I had a fantastic time."

"You're welcome. We'll definitely have to do this again."

Digging into one of the shopping bags, Lisa pulled out her new dangling earrings and clipped them to her earlobes. "I could go shopping every day!" she said with a hearty laugh.

"A girl after my own heart," Isabella answered. As she stared out the window, watching the storefronts on Vine Street whiz by, Isabella was relieved Lisa was finally coming out of her shell. She was much more relaxed

and talkative, and Isabella sensed Lisa was beginning to trust her. There was no doubt in
her mind that they were going to become
good friends.

"I don't want this day to end." Lisa sighed,
tilting her head against the backseat. "After
dinner why don't we go to the movies?"

Lisa's face was so open and hopeful that it
made Isabella shift uncomfortably in her seat.
"Maybe another night, Lisa. I'm going out
with my boyfriend, Danny, tonight. I'm sorry."

The bright smile shrank from Lisa's face,
and her stony expression returned. Without
saying another word, Lisa withdrew inside
herself, like a turtle sliding back inside its pro-
tective shell.

"And over here is where we edit the footage
and do voice-over work," Elizabeth said enthusiastically, leading Jessica and Josh to a small,
closet-size room right next to the WSVU studio. "We spend *a lot* of time in here."

Jessica inconspicuously pressed her fingers
to her mouth, trying to stifle a yawn. *If I don't
get out of here soon, I'm going to slip into a
coma,* she thought dully. What could possibly
be more boring than a tour of a college news-
room?

Apparently she was the only one who was
bored. Elizabeth chatted endlessly about the

drab little studio while Josh asked a ton of questions. His eyes narrowed and his lips were pinched together as he listened to Elizabeth talk, as if he were trying to memorize every word she was saying.

"How often do you broadcast?" he asked, scanning the spines of black videotape boxes lined up on the shelves.

Elizabeth folded her arms across her gray-and-blue WSVU News Team sweatshirt. Her perky blond ponytail bobbed up and down as she spoke. "We do two half-hour news shows—one at eight A.M. and one at six P.M.—and one-minute segments every hour on the hour."

"It sounds like you've got a tight schedule." Josh hooked his thumbs on the belt loops of his jeans and walked the perimeter of the studio.

"Actually it is." Elizabeth's brow crinkled and her lips were pulled back against her teeth. It was the face she always made whenever she talked about serious business. "The toughest thing is when nothing really happens. We have to generate a constant supply of fresh ideas for filler stories so we won't get stuck."

How about doing a piece on girlfriends who are bored out of their skulls? Jessica thought.

She wasn't used to having one of her boyfriends get along so well with her sister.

60

At one time Jessica longed for her twin's approval of the men she dated, but now she could see that having her sister's blessing was overrated. Insecurity tugged at the corners of her mind. Josh and Elizabeth seemed to have a lot in common—what if he started to like *her* instead?

Jessica stamped the heels of her sandals against the tile floor. Both Josh and Elizabeth looked up from the station's computer monitor, where she was showing him the script for that evening's news. "Sorry to break up the party, but it's time for us to get going," Jessica said edgily.

Immediately Josh stood up and extended his hand to Elizabeth. "Thanks for the tour—it was fun."

"Anytime," Elizabeth said with a smile. Her eyes widened suddenly, as if an idea had just come to her. "You know, Josh, Tom is supposed to go to a conference at the end of next week. He'll be gone for a couple of days and I could really use some help. Do you think you'd be up for it?"

Josh ran his hand through his long blond bangs. "I'd love to."

Jessica cleared her throat so loudly it burned. "Josh, darling, it's time to go."

"I'll give you a call, and we can make some arrangements," Elizabeth said.

"That sounds great," Josh said energetically. "I'll look forward to it."

"Hey there, stranger," Isabella said in a sultry voice as she opened the door to her apartment. Before Danny even had a chance to catch his breath from the five-floor climb up the stairs, Isabella wrapped her arms around his neck and kissed him passionately.

When they had finally run out of air, Danny pulled away, gasping. "Aren't you even going to invite me in?" he asked, his head feeling dizzy from the intensity of her kiss.

"I suppose so." Isabella pressed her lips against his for a second time, then yanked him into the apartment·by his necktie.

"You wouldn't happen to have a spare oxygen tank around here, would you?" Danny asked, breathing heavily. "I'm running a little short this evening."

"Why?" Isabella twirled around, showing off her red satin minidress and black strappy heels. As always, she looked incredible. "Am I that breathtaking?"

Danny caught her in his arms. "You could say that." Just as their lips were about to touch once more, Danny was startled by the sight of someone watching them. "Who is that?" he said in a low voice, pointing to the figure poking her head out from the spare bedroom.

"She's my new roommate—she's a little shy," Isabella whispered. She motioned for the young woman to come closer. "Lisa, why don't you come out and say hi to Danny?"

Shy wasn't the word that immediately came to Danny's mind—Lisa seemed utterly reclusive. Inch by inch, she crept her way out of the room like a garden snake. Danny smiled encouragingly as she approached. "It's nice to meet you, Lisa," he said, shaking her limp hand.

Lisa stared at him with frightened eyes. "Hi," she answered almost mechanically, her gaze fixed on him.

Danny tugged uncomfortably at the collar of his dress shirt. "How do you like the place so far?"

"It's nice." Lisa pushed the hair out of her eyes. Her cheeks were flushed. "Isabella took me shopping today."

"We had a great time," Isabella added, sliding her arm around Danny's waist. "Lisa bought some great clothes."

"I bought this and this," Lisa said, pointing to the jeans and sweater she was wearing.

"You look great." Danny didn't know what else to say.

Lisa's face turned a darker shade of crimson. "Thanks."

The fiery sparkle of the diamond ring on

Isabella's necklace suddenly reminded Danny of something. "Oh! I almost forgot," he said, snapping his fingers. "I brought you a present." He headed for the door.

Danny stepped out into the hallway to retrieve the decorated cardboard box he'd left near the door. Pangs of guilt had ached in his heart ever since the misunderstanding over the diamond ring. Isabella was a strong woman and had seemed to bounce back well from the disappointment, but Danny still felt bad. He wanted to do something special for her.

Isabella and Lisa exchanged curious looks. "What is it?" Isabella asked. Danny set the box on the table. "Open the box and check it out."

Isabella lifted the lid, and they all peered at the little black fur ball inside. "It's a kitten!" Isabella cooed.

"She was born three weeks ago," Danny said, carefully lifting the tiny creature out of the box and handing her to Isabella. "I thought you two could use another roommate."

The kitten was black all over, except for her white paws and a diamond-shaped spot between her deep black eyes. "What are we going to call you?" Isabella said in a baby voice as the kitten nuzzled her neck.

Lisa made no move toward the kitten. "I think we should name her Rosie," she said matter-of-factly.

Isabella held the kitten at eye level and stared at the little white spot. "You look like a Rosie, don't you?" She turned to Danny. "Maybe we shouldn't go dancing tonight—I'd hate to leave her alone on her first night in a strange place."

"I'm not going anywhere," Lisa said. "I'll look after her."

"As long as you don't mind." Isabella handed Rosie over to Lisa, whose thick, awkward hands held the kitten roughly. "Be gentle—she's fragile," Isabella said. "Thanks for taking care of her. On the way home Danny and I will pick up some food and a few toys."

"Have a great time," Lisa said, cradling the kitten in her arms.

"We should be back before midnight." Isabella threw a sheer chiffon wrap around her shoulders. "Don't wait up."

Danny opened the door for her and gave Lisa a friendly nod. "It was nice meeting you."

Lisa picked up one of Rosie's frosty white paws and waved it at Danny and Isabella. "Bye, Danny. Bye, Isabella."

As soon as the door was closed firmly behind them, Isabella planted a great big kiss on Danny's cheek. "Thanks for the kitten," she said as they walked past the broken elevator to the stairwell.

Danny's heart lightened. "Do you think Lisa liked it?"

Isabella nodded. "I think so—who wouldn't love something so adorable?"

"I wasn't talking about me," Danny said with a smirk. "I was talking about the kitten."

Isabella gave Danny a playful smack on his arm with her beaded evening bag. "So what's the verdict on Lisa?"

"I think she'll make a good roommate," Danny said as they stepped out the front door into the cool night air. "From what I can tell, you won't have to worry about Lisa throwing any wild parties—she's as tame as they come."

"What do you think, Rosie?" Lisa asked the kitten after Isabella and Danny left. "He's cute, isn't he?"

Rosie meowed softly, dark, frightened eyes looking up at her. Lisa bolted the door and glanced at the kitchen clock. It was only eight-thirty. The lonely evening stretched out before her like an endless black ribbon of road cutting through the desert.

"They're going dancing." Lisa sighed wistfully as she walked into the living room. Carrying the kitten firmly in her hands, Lisa's fingers curved around Rosie's tiny rib cage. The animal's fragile bones made Lisa think of delicate eggshells—the slightest pressure would be enough to crush them into splinters.

Lisa clicked on the stereo and searched the radio dial, holding Rosie in one hand. The kitten squirmed and scratched the air with her little white paws, trying to wriggle free.

"Do you like to dance?" Lisa asked Rosie, finding a station that played soft jazz music. "Would you like to be my partner?"

Lisa pressed the kitten against her cheek and swayed to the cool voice of Billie Holiday. Looking out the sliding glass doors that led to the balcony, Lisa saw Isabella and Danny with their arms wrapped around each other as they headed toward the parking lot.

What's it like to have such a great boyfriend? Lisa closed her eyes and moved in slow circles around the living room, imagining she was in a dark corner of a dance floor with Danny. She tried to imagine how it would feel to have his strong arms holding her, to have his body pressing against hers. *You are amazing, Lisa. You are the most incredible woman I have ever met . . .* he would whisper in her ear. She could almost feel his breath on her cheek.

A scorching trumpet solo pierced the emptiness in Lisa's heart. She danced on, her arms squeezing tighter and tighter. . . .

"Meow!" Rosie yelped, flailing wildly. The kitten leapt out of Lisa's arms and darted under the couch.

Reluctantly opening her eyes, Lisa was bitterly dragged back to the empty reality of the apartment. "Stupid cat," she hissed, clicking off the music.

Lisa plopped down hard on the couch, feeling the old springs sag beneath her weight. Leaning her head against the arm of the couch, Lisa noticed a rectangular wooden picture frame sitting on the telephone stand. She picked it up carefully, studying the photograph of a group of young women smiling brilliantly for the camera. They all had clear complexions and expensive clothes and looked as though they'd never wanted for anything in their whole lives. And in the center of the group was Isabella, outshining them all.

Perfect girl, perfect friends, perfect boyfriend, perfect life . . . The words ran through Lisa's mind like a chant as she stared at Isabella's smiling face. *Oh, Isabella. If only I could be you for just one day.*

Chapter
Five

Opening her mailbox, Isabella raised one eyebrow and shot Jessica a look of suspicion. "I don't believe you."

"I swear I'm telling you the truth!" Jessica insisted, tossing a stack of junk mail into the recycling bin. "Why would I lie about having a boyfriend?"

Isabella shrugged. "I don't know," she answered. The khaki linen vest and pants she was wearing, along with the leopard print scarf tied around her neck, made it look as if she'd just come back from a safari in the wilds of Africa. "But if he's all you say he is, then why are you hiding him from your friends? Is your mystery man a fugitive from the law?"

Weaving through the early Monday morning crowd, Jessica and Isabella made their way to the lounge of the student union. "For your information his name is Josh," Jessica said, pouncing on an oversize leather chair.

"At least I have a name," Isabella said dryly. "It's a start. Is Josh wanted in eight counties or did he cross state lines?"

Jessica giggled. "Do you honestly think I'd date a criminal?"

"Jessica, darling, I wouldn't put it past you."

A devilish look glimmered in Jessica's eye. "Well, I must say that it *does* sound kind of fun," she admitted. "So you really think I'm making him up?"

Isabella puckered her lips and blew gently on her morning coffee. "A few of us were beginning to wonder. After all, you've never been known for your subtlety."

"That settles it!" Jessica exclaimed with indignation. "You're meeting him tomorrow—I have a reputation to uphold!"

Isabella grinned. "So is he cute?"

Jessica sighed dreamily. "Stunning is a better word. He always looks like he's just stepped off the pages of a jeans ad. But I don't want to set up any expectations—you can judge for yourself tomorrow," she said. "The reason I've been so secretive is because Josh just transferred from UCLA and I know he's going to make a big splash when he starts classes tomorrow. There's no doubt in my mind that every girl on campus is going to want to sink her little claws into him."

Isabella rolled her sparkling gray eyes toward the ceiling. "I already told you—you have nothing to worry about from me."

"I know," Jessica answered, swinging her tanned legs over the arm of the leather chair. "But word gets around fast. I was lucky enough to meet him before most people, and I just wanted to make sure I had a running start."

"I'm still not sure I believe you," Isabella said, touching the scarf around her neck.

"You'll see for yourself tomorrow. Meet me in the coffeehouse at two o'clock. And bring your new roommate. I can't wait to meet her," Jessica said. "By the way, how's it going with her?"

"Even better than I thought it would," Isabella said honestly. "Surprisingly enough, I think we're becoming pretty good friends."

Lisa walked into the empty apartment, balancing a heavy bag full of groceries on one hip and stumbling across the linoleum floor in her new high heels. She'd spent the entire morning cruising the aisles of the local gourmet grocery store, trying to find something to make Isabella for lunch.

"I'll never get used to these stupid shoes,"

she thought aloud, sliding the pumps off her painfully swollen feet.

The smooth, cool floor felt good against the hot, itchy soles of Lisa's feet. Her finger traced the wormlike run in her brand-new nylons, starting from the hole in her big toe and crawling all the way up to her thigh. Lisa hiked up her knee-length skirt and pulled off her nylons, stuffing them into the trash can. Who would have thought that looking fashionable would be so physically demanding? Isabella always made it look effortless.

"Hi, Rosie." Lisa hummed happily. The tiny black kitten was curled up on the braided kitchen rug near the sink, sleeping peacefully in the warmth of a sunbeam. Lisa crouched down to pet the kitten, but Rosie scurried away frantically before she could even touch her. "Someone's grouchy today!" Lisa snorted.

Checking the wall clock, Lisa noticed it was eleven-fifty. According to the class schedule she had found in the top drawer of Isabella's desk, her psychology class was ending just about now. Lisa figured it would take Isabella just about five minutes to walk back to the apartment. *That doesn't leave much time to get lunch ready,* Lisa thought.

"It's a good thing there isn't a lot to do," Lisa said aloud as she emptied the grocery bag. She unwrapped the tomato, pesto, and mozzarella sandwiches she had bought and put them on a plate. They looked and smelled delicious. Lisa had never heard of pesto sandwiches before, but the other night, when she was brushing her teeth in the bathroom, she overheard Isabella talking on the phone to one of her friends. Isabella had mentioned she was craving a pesto sandwich, and Lisa had made note of it.

She'd been taking a lot of notes lately.

There was so much she wanted to learn from Isabella. Lisa had never met anyone so beautiful, so charming, so perfect. *If only I could be like her, my life would be perfect too.* Isabella didn't have any worries and nothing bad ever happened to her. *I want to be just like her.*

Quickly Lisa set the table, remembering the way Isabella had done it before. Taking Isabella's stemware out of the cupboard, Lisa poured two glasses of mineral water and set out two plates and cloth napkins. In the center of the table she placed a vase filled with freshly cut flowers.

Then the phone rang.

Lisa froze. *Should I pick it up?* she wondered. *What would I say?*

The phone rang several times until the answering machine turned on.

"Hi, Isabella, this is Danny . . ."

Lisa stared at the machine, entranced by the sound of Danny's deep voice. "Hi, Danny, this is Lisa," she whispered, even though she knew he couldn't hear her.

"It's just about noon, and I was wondering if you wanted to meet me for lunch in the dining hall. Call me as soon as you get in. I love you. Bye."

"Bye," Lisa answered. She frowned, looking at the elaborate spread on the table. A sinking feeling of disappointment invaded her as she thought of all the trouble she had gone through for Isabella, only to have it go to waste the second Danny called. It was her and Isabella's special time together, and Lisa didn't want anything or anyone to get in the way.

"Sorry, Danny," Lisa said out loud as she pressed the erase button on the answering machine. "You and Isabella will just have to get together some other time."

"What do you think you're doing?" Jessica shouted, shaking her wooden hairbrush threateningly at her sister. "I'm on to you, you know!"

Elizabeth looked up from her art history textbook and squinted at Jessica. "You can't be serious, Jess," she answered.

"I'm completely serious!" Jessica slammed the hairbrush on her vanity and stalked across

74

to Elizabeth's side of the room. Her blue-green eyes were icy cold.

Elizabeth giggled, softly at first, then louder until her shoulders shook convulsively. "I assure you, I'm not interested in your boyfriend."

Jessica clenched her jaw. What about the way Elizabeth bent over backward to show Josh the studio? Or how she always laughed at his jokes and smiled when he was around? Jessica knew heart-pounding attraction when she saw it.

"If you're not interested in Josh, then why did you offer him the job at the station?" Jessica argued with the confidence of a good prosecuting attorney. "*Especially* for the time when Tom is supposed to be away."

Elizabeth's laughter died and her face took on a weary expression. "I need the help, OK? And Josh seems like a great guy. Excuse me for being nice to my sister's boyfriend."

"You've never been nice to my boyfriends before."

"He's the first one who's actually worth being nice to," Elizabeth countered. She closed her art book. "What's gotten into you, anyway? Jessica Wakefield is rarely insecure."

Jessica folded her arms in front of her. "Don't change the subject, Liz. We're talking about your attraction to Josh."

"I'm not attracted to Josh," Elizabeth answered, wrinkling her nose. "He's too—" She stopped short.

The furious look on Jessica's face melted into a curious, brooding expression. She dropped her hands at her sides. "He's too what?"

Elizabeth's eyes were wide, as if she were about to explode. "Never mind," she suddenly said, turning back to her book.

Jessica leaned against the edge of her sister's desk and covered the page Elizabeth was reading with her hand. "Tell me."

"OK." Elizabeth exhaled, leaning back in her chair. "Josh is just a little too—pretty for my tastes."

"Pretty?" Jessica shook her head to make sure she'd heard right. "Did you just say *pretty?*"

Elizabeth nodded. "Yeah—you know, like those guys on the covers of romance novels with their tanned, muscular bodies and chiseled features. Or like an ancient Greek sculpture," she explained, pointing to an example in her art book. "Josh is amazing to look at, but he's too perfect."

"So you don't like him?" Jessica asked, her mouth turning down into a pout.

"He's just not my type," Elizabeth said. "I like someone who's a little more real. Crooked teeth and big ears give a person character."

Jessica's eyes were glassy. She stared off into space as though she'd just heard some devastating news. It was completely beyond her comprehension that someone might not find Josh attractive. She didn't know whether to feel relieved or offended. "Honestly, Liz, you wouldn't know a gorgeous guy if he came up and hit you over the head!"

Elizabeth shook her head in disbelief. "First you accuse me of trying to steal your boyfriend, then you get mad when I tell you I don't like him!" She leaned over her desk and returned to her studying. "If you're going to act that way when you introduce Josh to your friends, I suggest you keep him in hiding forever!"

"What's all this?" Isabella asked as she walked through the door of the apartment. Hanging her shoulder bag on the coatrack, she stared at the beautifully set table and the delicious-looking food. "Are we having a party?"

A barefooted Lisa was standing by the sink expectantly, dressed in her new black skirt and sweater. The skirt could have used some ironing and she definitely needed a pair of nylons and some shoes, but Lisa still looked much better than she did two days before. Her tangled hair was pulled back in a tortoiseshell barrette, and she was wearing just enough makeup to take the edge off her usually pale skin. "It's for you," Lisa said modestly. "I thought you might be hungry."

Isabella's glossy red lips curved into a beautiful smile. "Actually I'm starved. Lunch looks fabulous." Her eyes darted instinctively to the answering machine, but the red light wasn't blinking. No messages.

"Danny didn't call for me, did he?"

"No," Lisa answered shortly as she took a seat at the table. "I hope you like tomato, mozzarella, and pesto sandwiches—that's what I got."

"They're my favorite," Isabella said distractedly, picking up the phone.

Lisa stared at her. "What are you doing?"

"Calling Danny." Isabella dialed the number.

"Everything's ready right now, so why don't you call him after you eat?" Lisa suggested with a strained smile.

Isabella's gray eyes narrowed as she watched tension lines appear around Lisa's mouth. After all the trouble she'd gone to, it would be rude to ruin her plans. "OK." She hung up the phone and returned to the kitchen. "I'll call him later."

"Great." Lisa's features lightened and the lines disappeared. "Save room for dessert," she instructed, pointing to the plate of miniature pastries sitting on the counter.

Isabella draped a cloth napkin across her lap, dumbfounded by the unbelievable metamorphosis Lisa had undergone in just a few days. "This is wonderful, Lisa," she said, biting into the luscious sandwich. "How did you find time to do all this on your first day of classes?"

Carefully Lisa unfolded her napkin and placed it in her lap. "Actually my classes didn't start today after all. The registrar's office lost my schedule and won't be able to generate a new one until the end of the week. They can't even tell me what classes I'm supposed to be in."

"That's the strangest thing I've ever heard," Isabella said indignantly. She dabbed the corners of her mouth with the napkin. "If you want me to go down there and straighten it out for you, let me know."

"No—that's all right," Lisa barked, pulling off a bite-size piece of bread and popping it into her mouth. "I don't mind having the week off anyway. It gives me more time to go shopping."

A little black fur ball came bounding out from underneath the couch and curled itself around Isabella's ankle. "Hi there, Rosie," Isabella cooed. She fed Rosie a piece of cheese and the kitten meowed, contentedly rubbing her back against Isabella's legs. "By the way, Lisa, you look great."

Lisa blushed a deep red. "Thanks." She

touched the back of her head self-consciously. "I didn't know what to do with my hair, so I just stuck it in a barrette."

"I used to wear my hair the same way—when I had long hair." Isabella took another bite of sandwich.

"Really?" Lisa sipped her mineral water, her eyes suddenly distant. "Isabella—can I ask you a personal question?"

She looked at Lisa with curiosity. "What is it?"

Lisa's brow creased, and an intense look darkened her hazel eyes. "What's it like to have a boyfriend?"

A nervous laugh escaped Isabella's throat, but Lisa's serious expression made her stop short. Even though Lisa had to be at least eighteen, sometimes Isabella felt as if she were living with a child. "What do you want to know?"

Lisa shrugged, looking down at her plate. "What's it like when you're with Danny?"

Putting down her sandwich, Isabella gave the question some thought. "It's wonderful, most of the time," she said. "We laugh a lot and have fun together. We talk about things that bother us."

Isabella's words had a false ring to her own ears. Yes, she did have an incredible time when she was with Danny, but she hadn't always told him when something was bothering her. Especially the whole situation about the ring. Isabella had somehow convinced herself that it wasn't a big deal that Danny didn't want to marry her right now, but a quiet, persistent voice in the back of her mind kept telling her that he really didn't love her. If Danny loved her, Isabella reasoned, he wouldn't give it a second thought. He'd marry her in a heartbeat.

Lisa leaned forward on her elbows, seemingly enraptured by what Isabella had to say. "What's the best thing about your relationship?"

"I guess it's the fact that he knows me so well," Isabella answered, wincing as she spoke. This was the answer she used to give when someone asked her. But she was beginning to wonder if she was only deluding herself. "Most of the time I don't even have to say a word and Danny knows exactly what I'm thinking."

"That sounds cool," Lisa said. "And what's bad about it?"

That was an easy one. Isabella took a long drink of water. "When your goals and expectations are different. Sometimes you have to compromise. You can't always think of yourself—you have to think about the other person's happiness."

Lisa resumed eating her sandwich. "I've never had a boyfriend."

"You mean a serious one?" Isabella asked.

"I've never even been on a *date* before," Lisa said flatly.

Even though Lisa didn't seem particularly distressed by this fact, Isabella was blown away. "Why not?"

Lisa licked a bit of pesto off her fingers. "I never had the chance to where I grew up. My parents always kept me under lock and key."

"That's terrible."

Lisa grinned awkwardly. "I don't care all that much. Dating and relationships just seem like a big pain."

The more Isabella found out about Lisa's past, the more intrigued she became. "Tell me," Isabella began with intense interest. "What's your family like?"

Lisa's smile evaporated. "You know, the usual," she answered evasively.

Unsatisfied, Isabella pressed further. "Do you have any brothers or sisters?"

Lisa's eyes fell. "I had a twin sister, but she died at birth. My parents didn't have any more children after that."

Isabella's heart ached. She couldn't imagine how devastating it would be to lose a twin. "I'm so sorry," she said quietly.

Tossing her napkin casually on the table,

Lisa managed a smile. "I told you something personal about me, now it's your turn again," she said lightly. "What was it like for you growing up?"

"I guess I had a pretty happy childhood," Isabella admitted. "My father is an architect and my mother works for a fashion designer. Both my parents are incredibly creative and fun to be around, but I'm an only child. Growing up, I always wondered what it would be like to have a sibling."

"Which did you want? A brother or sister?"

Gazing out through the sliding glass doors, Isabella's eyes focused on a patch of blue sky. "I guess I've always wanted a younger sister— you know, someone to talk about boys or to go places with. Someone I could teach things to."

Lisa nodded. "I know what you mean."

Isabella and Lisa stared at each other for a moment. *She does understand what I mean,* Isabella thought. She felt a deep bond between them taking root. If they each longed for a sister, then they could be pseudosisters to each other. Lisa needed companionship and guidance, and Isabella needed someone to take care of and guide. Isabella longed to be the sister Lisa never had.

"Maybe we could pretend to be sisters," Lisa suggested, verbalizing Isabella's thoughts.

"We won't tell anyone. It'd just be between you and me."

Isabella smiled. "I'd like that," she said. "What are you doing tomorrow?"

"Nothing." Lisa's expression was hopeful.

"I'm meeting a friend of mine at the coffee-house at two o'clock. Do you want to come along?" Isabella asked.

Lisa grinned. "I'd love to, sis."

Chapter
Six

"What took you so long?" Jessica teased Isabella in between sips of raspberry seltzer. "I was getting lonely."

Isabella scanned the empty tables of the coffeehouse. The midday lull had set in as many students headed to their afternoon classes. "Where's your man?" she asked.

"He'll be here soon," Jessica answered with confidence.

Isabella stepped aside to pull up an extra chair from a nearby table. "Jessica, I'd like you to meet my new roommate, Lisa." Isabella motioned toward a young woman standing directly behind her.

"Hi, Lisa," Jessica said warmly, extending her hand. "It's nice to meet you."

"Hi," Lisa answered, offering a slightly limp handshake. She was wearing a cotton poet's shirt and a black skirt, and her hair was rolled into a chignon. Simple and understated, but elegant. "I've heard a lot about you."

Jessica gave her hair a playful, haughty flip. "You can't believe everything you hear," she joked, batting her eyes.

Lisa giggled, covering her mouth shyly. "They were all good things."

A playful smirk twisted Jessica's lips. "Like I said, you can't believe everything you hear."

Watching Lisa take the seat next to her, Jessica couldn't help being a little amazed. Isabella had described Lisa as introverted and unattractive, but Jessica found her to be the exact opposite. Although she was quiet, Lisa seemed engaging and interesting, and as far as style was concerned, she reminded Jessica a lot of Isabella. Not only were her clothes similar, but her gestures were as well. If she didn't know better, Jessica would have thought they were related.

"I'm ready for my midday caffeine fix." Isabella raised her arm in the air to get the waitress's attention. Despite the lack of customers, the waitresses ignored Isabella's attempts at getting their attention. "This is ridiculous," Isabella said in frustration.

Lisa's eyes narrowed. "What do you want, Isabella?"

"Just a cappuccino—but it doesn't matter. It's not worth the trouble."

Without warning, Lisa stood up and glared at the coffee bar. She leaned forward, pressing her palms on the tabletop like an army general in a war room. "What does it take to get service around here?" she shouted in a clear, assertive voice.

The waitresses' conversation stopped suddenly, their startled eyes searching to see where the voice came from. Isabella and Jessica exchanged looks of surprise.

"Over here," Lisa said, waving her arm at them. Her jaw was set and her eyes hard. "Two cappuccinos—*right now!*"

The waitresses scurried in every direction, running into one another as if they were competing in a race to see who could get the order ready the fastest.

A shocked giggle escaped Isabella's throat. "Thanks, Lisa," she said, brushing the lint off her tweed blazer and tan riding pants. Her brown leather riding boots gleamed under the soft overhead lights. "We probably would've waited forever."

"Good going," Jessica said, giving Lisa an encouraging pat on the back. "It's about time someone put those snobs in their place."

Lisa slid back onto her chair, the hard lines of her face gradually dissolving. "I didn't like their attitude, that's all," she answered in a low voice.

Lisa is definitely an interesting person, Jessica decided as she sipped her seltzer. She had only known Lisa for five minutes, and already she was dying to know more. "How do you like SVU, Lisa?"

Lisa crossed her legs and rested her folded hands in her lap. "So far it seems really great, but I haven't been out too much."

"Izzy and I will take care of that," Jessica answered, nodding in Isabella's direction.

Isabella ran her fingers through her short hair. "We know all the campus hot spots."

"And all the *off*-campus ones too," Jessica added.

One of the waitresses raced over to their table, setting down two glass mugs of foamy coffee. "Um . . . sorry about the delay," she stammered.

"Don't let it happen again," Jessica snarled, winking at Lisa.

Isabella's eyes focused on something in the distance, a look of astonishment slowly coming over her face like the break of dawn. Suddenly she jumped up. "What are you doing here?" Isabella said excitedly.

Lisa and Jessica turned to see Isabella locked in a clinch with someone other than Danny. Jessica's jaw fell open when she recognized the tall, lean frame, the sun-bleached hair, the smoky blue eyes. It was Josh.

"I guess you two don't need any introductions," Jessica said dryly, noting how Isabella couldn't tear herself away from Josh's piercing blue eyes. Jealousy gnawed ferociously at Jessica's insides.

Isabella laughed. "We went to high school together."

"We dated for a year, to be more specific," Josh said, his arms still clinging to Isabella's shoulders.

"Ten months," Isabella corrected. Her face was glowing. "It was only ten months."

Lisa looked impressed. "You two dated?"

"High-school sweethearts," Jessica said, stretching a taut smile across her face until she thought it would crack. "What a strange coincidence!"

"How have you been, Josh?" Isabella asked, looking him up and down for a third time. "You look fabulous!"

"Great," he answered. Jessica wondered when the nauseating look of amazement was going to fade from his eyes. "I just transferred from UCLA—I completely forgot that you were here."

Yeah, right, Jessica thought. Her stomach clenched into a tight ball. She pushed her raspberry seltzer to the side. The thought of eating or drinking anything at that moment made her sick.

Isabella hugged Josh again, with a little too much enthusiasm as far as Jessica was concerned. "If you'd kept in touch, you would've remembered."

Jessica waited for Isabella and Josh to finally untangle themselves before throwing herself into his arms. "Hi there, big guy. Remember me?"

Josh kissed Jessica affectionately on the forehead. "Sorry I'm late—I got hung up after class," he explained, sitting in the empty chair next to her. Hanging his jean jacket on the back of the chair, Josh shook his head in disbelief. "I still can't believe you're here, Isabella. You look great."

"Doesn't she?" Jessica interjected with false enthusiasm. *This is so weird,* she thought. What were the chances that she'd start dating one of Isabella's old flames? One in a million? Every time Jessica thought about how happy Josh and Isabella were to see each other, she wanted to curl up in a corner and die. *Isabella is madly in love with Danny,* Jessica reasoned with herself. *Don't get bent out of shape.*

"Josh, I'd like you to meet my roommate, Lisa," Isabella said, motioning to Lisa, who was inconspicuously sipping her coffee. "Lisa, this is Josh."

"Hi, Lisa," Josh answered, waving at her casually.

Lisa's face burned scarlet, her eyes glued to the tabletop. "Hi," she whispered.

The cloud of jealousy lifted momentarily as Jessica watched Lisa suddenly become over-taken by painful shyness. It was obvious that she hadn't spent much time around guys, espe-cially ones as gorgeous as Josh. "Lisa's a trans-fer student too," Jessica said.

"Oh yeah?" Josh's eyebrows raised a frac-tion of an inch. "Where are you from?"

Lisa didn't answer. Instead she stole quick glances in Josh's direction, then turned her head away.

"New York," Isabella said, coming to her rescue. "She went to NYU."

"That's cool." Josh took a drink from Jessica's raspberry seltzer. "I love New York."

Isabella reached across the table and touched Josh lightly on the arm. "Whenever you get settled and you have some free time, I'd love for us to get together. We have a lot to catch up on."

"I'd like that too," he said, standing up. He grabbed his jacket. "I wish we could talk right now, but I have a meeting in about five min-utes."

Jessica pouted, feeling neglected. "You're leaving already?"

"I have to meet with my new adviser," Josh answered gently. Then he cupped Jessica's face in his hands and kissed her with such ardor that any trace of insecurity she still had evaporated.

"Am I going to see you tonight?" Jessica asked with a languid smile, her head reeling from his kiss.

Josh brushed the hair out of her blue-green eyes. "I'll call you after dinner," he promised. "Maybe we can go to the movies."

"Sounds great," Jessica said. All of a sudden her dreamy expression turned into a scowl. "Shoot! I forgot—I can't see you tonight. I'm supposed to baby-sit for my professor's kids."

Josh's shoulders slumped in disappointment. "I'll give you a call anyway, before you go," he answered glumly, picking up his books. He waved to Isabella and Lisa. "I'll see you around."

All three women watched with admiration as he walked out of the coffeehouse. Jessica sulked over her drink. "Stupid baby-sitting job!" she said heavily.

Lisa raised her head for the first time since Josh arrived. "If you want, I could take the job for you."

"I need the money too much," Jessica said dismissively. "But thanks anyway."

"I'll give you half," Lisa offered.

Jessica dropped her straw. "Really?"

Lisa nodded.

Isabella's eyes narrowed. "I don't mean to get in the middle of this, but it doesn't seem like a great idea to me," she said. "Lisa, you shouldn't give up half the money if you're doing all the work."

"She's right," Jessica admitted sullenly. "It's not really fair."

Lisa shrugged. "I don't mind. I have nothing to do tonight anyway, so if I get a little money for it, all the better."

The gears in Jessica's head started turning. Having Lisa do the baby-sitting was the ideal situation—Jessica could go out *and* get some money too, without lifting a finger. But even Jessica had to admit that it wasn't cool to take advantage of Lisa.

"If you two will excuse me, I have to go pick up my Range Rover at the garage. It's finally ready," Isabella said, slinging her little brown purse over her shoulder. She turned to Lisa. "If Danny calls for me, please tell him where I am."

"Sure thing," Lisa answered.

Isabella smiled at Jessica. "You were right about your new boyfriend—he's a great guy."

"I bet Danny would think so too," Jessica said slyly.

Isabella sighed. "My dating Josh in high school doesn't change anything," she insisted. "I still love Danny very much—and besides, you're my best friend. I would never steal your boyfriend away from you."

Deep in her heart Jessica knew that Isabella wasn't capable of betrayal, but she still needed the reassurance. She reached over and gave Isabella a grateful hug. "Thanks, Iz."

Isabella said good-bye to both of them, then disappeared behind the plastic palm tree near the exit. Lisa looked down at her cappuccino, her short pink-polished fingertips tracing circles around the edge of the mug. "I can't believe they used to date each other," she said when Isabella was out of earshot.

"Me neither." Jessica tried to ignore the tightness that lingered in her stomach. "But that's all in the past. It doesn't matter anymore."

Lisa nodded thoughtfully. "I wonder why they broke up. And who was the one to end it."

That's exactly what I was thinking, Jessica mused. Secretly she hoped that Josh had been the one to break up with Isabella. Then she'd know that he wasn't interested in Isabella anymore. But if it was the other way around, there was the threat that Josh was carrying a torch for Isabella.

"If I had a guy like that, I'd keep my eye on him every minute," Lisa said. "If you still want to go out with Josh tonight, I'll baby-sit for you. Think about it."

It took less than half a second for Jessica to make up her mind. "Can you be there by eight?"

"How was your day, Rosie?" Lisa said in a cheerful, singsong voice as she returned to the apartment. The tiny kitten sat next to her gigantic dish of cat food, ignoring Lisa as she playfully batted the morsels of food with her paws.

Lisa threw her keys heavily onto the table, the sound echoing in the empty kitchen. "That good, huh?" she said to the unresponsive kitten. Lisa knelt down beside her on the linoleum. "Come here, Rosie." She made clicking sounds with her tongue.

Rosie looked at her with big, black eyes. Lisa kicked off her high heels with a forceful snap of her toes, sending the shoes skittering across the floor. Rosie hopped out of the way, watching as the shoes slammed into the dish, sending cat food flying through the air.

"I had a great day. I met some *fabulous* new friends." Lisa strutted over to the living room. She practiced her new way of walking— chin high, shoulders back, one foot carefully placed in front of the other—just the way she had seen Isabella do it.

The phone rang. "That's probably my new friend Jessica," Lisa informed Rosie, who had disappeared into the safety of Isabella's bedroom. Lisa lunged for the phone. "Hello?"

"Lisa? This is Danny."

"Hi, Danny," Lisa said, her gravelly voice melting into pure sugar. She stretched out on the couch with her feet propped up on the armrest. "How are you?"

"Fine," Danny answered curtly. He sounded as if he had something urgent on his mind. "Is Isabella there?"

Lisa twirled the phone cord around her fingers. "No—she hurried off somewhere a few hours ago."

Danny sighed. "I've been calling all morning. And she never returned my phone call from yesterday."

"I'm sorry, Danny," Lisa said sympathetically. "It must be tough to have a girlfriend who's busy all the time."

"It's pretty frustrating," Danny answered.

Lisa's stomach did a flip. *Danny's actually having a conversation with me,* she thought ecstatically. *The nicest, most gorgeous man I've ever met is actually having a conversation with me.* Lisa fought to keep her poise. "I can imagine," she answered.

"Do you have any idea where she might be? I really need to talk to her."

If Danny calls for me, please tell him where I am, Isabella had said at the coffeehouse. But Lisa couldn't tell Danny—at least not right away. The longer she waited, the longer he'd stay on the line, talking to her. "I saw Isabella a few hours ago in the coffeehouse," she said. "While we were there, the funniest thing happened."

"What was that?" Danny asked.

Lisa looked dreamily at the ceiling, savoring Danny's attention. He was hanging on her every word. "We were just sitting there, drinking coffee with Jessica, when all of a sudden one of Isabella's old boyfriends walked in."

"Who is he?" Danny said, with more than a hint of interest in his voice.

"His name is Josh—he just transferred here," Lisa said innocently. "They went out for about a year in high school. Even though it's been a few years since they've seen each other, they hit it off so well, you'd think they dated last week."

"Huh . . ." Danny was quiet for a moment. "Do you think they're together right now?"

"No, I doubt it," Lisa answered. "Josh left the coffeehouse alone, then Isabella left about a minute later."

"Could you have her call me?"

"Absolutely," Lisa answered. She could tell Danny was worried, and the thought of it sent a curious thrill through her. "I'll have her call you as soon as she gets in."

"This afternoon has been a *total* nightmare!" Isabella slammed the door behind her and threw her purse impatiently on the kitchen table. She walked into the living room, where Lisa was, and flung herself on an easy chair. "When I got to the garage, it turned out that they weren't completely finished with the Rover after all. The mechanic who was working on it went home sick. So I sat around waiting for two hours. A woman in the waiting room spilled coffee all over my riding pants." She pointed to the dark spot that covered her knee. "Then when the Rover was finally ready, no one could find my keys." She stopped to take a breath. "Guess where they were?"

Lisa, who was stretched out on the couch, reading a fashion magazine, looked up and shrugged. "I have no idea."

"They were in the sick mechanic's pocket!" Isabella threw her arms up in the air in exasperation. "He'd forgotten to leave them at the shop. The guy was too sick to bring them back to the garage, so I had to wait until his wife came home from work so she could bring them. On top of all that, the total cost was a hundred dollars over the estimate."

Lisa shook her head sympathetically. "That's really terrible, Isabella. I'm sorry that happened to you."

"You're not the only one who's sorry." Isabella's tired eyes rested on the kitchen clock. It was seven-thirty. She groaned.

Danny was probably wondering where she was. "Did Danny call?"

"About three hours ago," Lisa answered, closing the thick magazine. She stretched her arms above her head and yawned. "He sounded really mad."

"Great," Isabella answered sourly. She wasn't in the mood to have it out with Danny too. "What was he mad about?"

"He said he'd been trying to reach you all morning and you weren't around. And he was wondering why you didn't call him yesterday."

"*He* was the one who was supposed to call *me* yesterday and he never did. What am I supposed to do? Check in with him every hour?" Isabella's bad mood darkened. "Am I being unreasonable or are men totally insane?"

Lisa slipped on her new sneakers and tied the laces. "Sounds to me like you have every right to be mad. Danny seems kind of demanding."

"Thank you," Isabella said with a firm nod. Danny had already made it clear that he didn't want a serious commitment—he had no right to act as if he owned her.

"I don't know much about relationships, but if I were you, I wouldn't call him back." Lisa put on her windbreaker. "Just so he gets the message that you're not on call twenty-four hours a day."

"Good idea," Isabella answered. It was good to have an impartial opinion, especially when it was in her favor. She watched as Lisa got ready to go out. "Where are you going?"

"I'm baby-sitting for Jessica," Lisa explained.

"She's not taking half, is she?"

Lisa shook her head. "I get to keep it all."

Isabella smiled with approval. "I'm just looking out for my sister."

Lisa smiled. "I'll see you tomorrow," she said before closing the door behind her.

Chapter
Seven

"Jessica, what are you doing here?" Josh opened his door a crack, just enough to stick his head out. He was bare chested, with a towel wrapped around his waist, and his blue eyes were wide with surprise. "I thought I was supposed to call you around eight."

"I wanted to see you now." Jessica craned her neck to try to see over Josh's shoulder, but his body blocked the doorway.

"This isn't the best time . . . ," he began.

A cold, prickly sensation ran down Jessica's spine. She had the feeling that Josh was definitely hiding something. Was it another woman? Isabella? "We need to talk," she insisted.

"Can you give me five minutes?"

And give her time to escape out the window? No way. A sudden rush of anger bubbled inside

Jessica. How could Isabella and Josh do this to her?

"We need to talk, *now*," Jessica answered as she shoved open the door.

Josh scampered around the room, throwing on a thin cotton bathrobe. "What's so urgent that it can't wait until after I take my shower?"

Opening the closet door and checking under the bed, Jessica gave the room a thorough search. When she was satisfied that Josh was alone, the surge of jealousy subsided, leaving her feeling foolish.

"What is it?" he repeated.

Since I'm here, I might as well say something. Jessica smiled weakly. "It's about you and Isabella."

"What about me and Isabella?" His look of impatience melted into curiosity.

Jessica sat down on the edge of his bed. "Were you two in love when you went out?"

Josh folded his arms across his broad chest. His brow wrinkled as though he wasn't sure he'd heard her right. "It was a while ago—but I think we were," he answered. "Why?"

Jessica ignored Josh's question, firing another one at him instead. "Whose idea was it to break up?"

"Hers, but—"

"So you're still in love with her?" Jessica accused.

"No—not at all." Josh gently held her by the shoulders. "What's gotten into you?"

Jessica looked deep into Josh's eyes. "It was a big shock to discover that my best friend and my boyfriend once dated. I'm sorry if I'm not handling it so well."

Josh knelt down so they were at eye level and took her hands in his. "It was a surprise for me too," he explained. "I didn't mean to make you feel bad. It was great seeing Isabella again, but you have to believe me when I say that I'm crazy about *you*. Whatever Isabella and I had is long gone."

Jessica wanted desperately to believe him, but doubts continued to tug at the corners of her mind. Relationships were always much more fragile than people seemed to think. "But she's the one who broke up with you— what if she decides she wants to get back together?"

"Listen to me," Josh said softly. He moved closer until she could feel his warm breath on her cheek. "Isabella and I aren't getting back together. It's over. One of the things I always admired about Isabella was how loyal she was to her friends. She'd never do anything to break us up."

Once again jealousy had clouded Jessica's vision, making her forget what a wonderful friend Isabella had been to her. She smiled sheepishly at Josh. "And you don't want to get together with her again?"

Josh pressed his soft lips against hers in a lingering kiss. "Does that answer your question?"

Jessica nodded, grinning. "I suppose I should go so you can get ready," she said, playing with the lapels of his robe.

"You'd better," he said. "I have a hot date tonight, and I want to make sure I look good."

"Who is she?" Jessica teased.

Josh rubbed his chin thoughtfully. "A bright, beautiful, incredibly interesting woman who I'm crazy about."

"She sounds much too good for you," Jessica said jokingly.

Josh tenderly kissed the tip of her nose. "I was thinking the exact same thing."

Isabella rolled wearily onto her back, clutching a pillow to her chest. She closed her eyes as her limbs sank into the cushions of the couch as if they were being pressed with lead weights. It had been an impossibly draining day, and as much as she needed to hear the reassuring voice of her boyfriend, Isabella was afraid they'd only end up in a huge fight if she called.

Just as she was drifting off to sleep the phone rang. Instinctively she reached for it, too submerged in a dreamy haze to think clearly.

Danny's voice boomed on the other end. "Where have you been?"

Isabella's dark mood returned. "Hello to you too."

"You didn't call me yesterday—I was worried."

"You were supposed to call *me*," she retorted.

"I did," he said. "I left a message on your answering machine."

Isabella's head pounded. "There weren't any messages on the machine when I came home."

"Where did you come home *from?*" Danny probed.

"I don't remember—class, I guess," Isabella said, raising her voice. "And today I spent the entire afternoon at the garage, waiting for my car to be fixed. Are you satisfied? Or do you need a few eyewitnesses?"

"I already have a few," Danny said angrily. "What were you doing before you went to the garage?"

Isabella's cheeks flushed with frustration. "What is this? An FBI interrogation?"

"Just answer the question. . . ."

"Don't you trust me at all?" Isabella asked incredulously. She took a deep breath to clear the pounding in her head. "Look," she said, struggling to keep her voice even, "I've had a pretty rough day and I'm not in the mood to argue. Let's talk about this tomorrow."

"I need to see you tonight," Danny insisted.

The sorry tone in his voice disarmed her. "I miss you. I don't want to argue either, but we definitely need to talk."

Isabella sighed. "Meet me at the snack bar in fifteen minutes."

This day can't get much worse, Isabella thought miserably as she hung up the phone. It wasn't bad enough that she had to spend a grueling afternoon trying to get her car back, but now Danny was mad at her and she wasn't even sure why. He wasn't acting like himself—it was unusual for him to be so possessive. Whatever was bothering him, she hoped it would soon pass.

Dragging herself off the couch, Isabella made her way across the seemingly endless living room to her bedroom to change out of her stained pants. She slipped on a pair of her favorite blue jeans, eyeing her comfortable bed with longing. As soon as she was done talking to Danny she was going to crash.

"I'd better wear my pullover," Isabella thought aloud, remembering the chilly breeze she had felt when she came in. She turned on the closet light and quickly flipped through the hangers. It wasn't there.

"Where could it be?" she said. She remembered mentioning to Lisa that she could borrow her clothes whenever she wanted—maybe it was in her closet.

Isabella stepped through their adjoining bathroom and into Lisa's room. The room was still as empty as it had been when Lisa first moved in except for the addition of a green scatter rug, a few decorative pillows on the futon, and some simple curtains. Isabella was glad to see that Lisa was settling in.

As she opened the closet door Isabella was surprised to see the once-empty closet nearly filled to capacity. "Lisa must've done a lot of shopping in the last few days," she said to herself. Isabella reached in, putting her hands on the burgundy chambray shirt she had bought a few months ago with Jessica. It was one of her favorites. While Isabella didn't mind Lisa borrowing some of her clothes, she wished she'd at least return them when she was done. Isabella took the shirt off the hanger and draped it over her arm.

Behind the blouse was a silver slip dress Isabella had bought for one of the Theta parties. "Why would she want to borrow this?" Isabella snatched the dress off the hanger with irritation. Behind the dress were her palazzo pants. One by one Isabella went through the entire closet, discovering that virtually everything inside it belonged to her.

I'm going to have to have a talk with Lisa, Isabella thought bitterly as she finally found her Southwest print pullover at the back of the closet. There was a limit to how many things you could borrow from someone without asking. Obviously Lisa had no sense of what that limit was.

"Great, now I'm late." Danny would probably be mad about that too. Isabella stomped back to her room. She flung open her closet door and was starting to hang up the clothes Lisa had borrowed when suddenly she froze.

Her pullover was hanging on the back of the door.

"It can't be . . ." Isabella looked up at the pullover on the hook and then down at the one in her arms. They were identical.

Impulsively Isabella dropped the pile of clothes at her feet and started rummaging through her own closet. The burgundy shirt, the silver slip dress, the palazzo pants were all there—hanging right where she had left them—exact duplicates of the clothes she'd found in Lisa's closet.

"What's going on here?" Isabella cupped her hand over her mouth in disbelief. "Why would she do something like this?"

"It's so weird, Danny. Why would Lisa buy the exact same clothes I have?" Isabella's normally bright eyes looked hazy and distant. She didn't seem like herself at all as she sat in one of the snack bar booths, nervously tearing at the corners of a paper napkin.

Danny leaned forward on his elbows, watching Isabella. She seemed distraught about something, and a wrenching feeling in Danny's gut told him it had nothing to do with Lisa borrowing clothes. He had a hunch Josh was the one who was on Isabella's mind.

"Don't you think it's strange?"

"Haven't you heard that imitation is the sincerest form of flattery?" Danny remarked offhandedly. He had no desire to delve into Lisa's motivations, knowing full well that Isabella was only making conversation as a smoke screen. The real issue at hand was that an old boyfriend was back in Isabella's life.

Isabella continued to shred the napkin into tiny, confettilike pieces. "I think there's more to it. Maybe she has psychological problems."

"Don't be so judgmental," Danny answered, but his mind was somewhere else entirely, back to earlier in the day when he had spoken to Lisa. *They hit it off so well, you'd think they dated last week,* she'd said. Danny's heart ached at the thought of Isabella being interested in someone else.

Isabella's cheeks flushed nearly as red as her crimson lips. "How am I being judgmental?"

"I don't know," Danny said heavily. It was too painful to look into her eyes, so he watched the line of students at the snack counter. "I just don't think Lisa would be too happy if she knew you were snooping around in her closet."

"I wasn't snooping." Isabella's voice took on an angry edge. "I was looking for my sweater."

The conversation degenerated, and Danny felt as though he were sinking through quicksand, with nothing to grasp to pull himself out. Why were they arguing over something so meaningless? "Can we please drop the subject?"

"It figures—just because it's important to me, you want to drop the subject." Isabella grabbed a fresh napkin from the dispenser and tore it to shreds.

Danny opened his mouth to respond, but nothing came out. Instead he looked at her blankly, wondering desperately what thoughts were running wildly around inside her head. Was she thinking about Josh?

Danny swallowed hard. "Tell me about your day."

"It was completely hellish," Isabella said, her mouth pinched into a scowl.

Here's your chance, a little voice coaxed inside Danny's head. *Ask her about Josh.* His muscles contracted as he prepared for the worst. "When I talked to Lisa on the phone, she said you ran into an old boyfriend of yours."

The tense expression on Isabella's face relaxed. "Josh," she answered calmly. "We dated in high school, and out of the blue he transferred here. Now he's dating Jessica," she explained. "It's an incredible coincidence—and it was great to see him."

"How great was it?" Without his thinking, the words burst out of Danny's mouth and hung uncomfortably in the air.

Isabella stared at him oddly, as though he were an old acquaintance she'd run into on the street whom she didn't recognize. "What's your point, Danny?" she said icily.

This is getting worse by the minute, he thought. "Lisa mentioned that you two hit it off pretty well." He spoke casually, trying to take the edge off. "I was just wondering if it was like old times."

Isabella ravaged another napkin, adding to the growing pile of litter on the table. "If you're wondering if I kissed him, you're way off base."

"I—I didn't say that," Danny stammered.

"You might as well have," she retorted. Her eyes were ablaze. "Thanks for having so little faith in me and in our relationship!"

Before Danny could answer, Isabella stood up and stormed out.

The following morning Isabella sat on a

111

bench in the student union, eating the last of a blueberry muffin and feeling completely miserable. She watched students pass by on their way to class, hoping to catch a glimpse of Danny. Her eyes darted hopefully from one end of the large, open foyer to the other, but he was nowhere in sight.

I was too hard on him last night, she thought, brushing the last bit of crumbs from her brown suede skirt. Even though Danny had seemed a little insecure about Josh, the clarity of early morning allowed Isabella to see that she had overreacted. Frustration at the garage had turned her mood into a swelling monster that devoured everyone in its path— including Danny and Lisa.

Now that her head was clear and her mood calm, Isabella vowed to make things right again. First she'd start with Danny. Ever since the misunderstanding with the ring, she'd been harboring feelings of hurt and disappointment. As much as she tried to deny them, they wouldn't go away. It wasn't fair to keep her feelings a secret from Danny. It was time to let him know how she felt.

Picking up her things, Isabella threw the muffin wrapper in the trash can and walked down the long hallway toward the campus bookstore. *I'll buy him a cute card—that should set everything back on track,* she thought,

112

smiling to herself. Later they'd have to talk.

Then, of course, there was Lisa. Isabella cringed when she thought of the hostile way she had reacted when Danny told her she was being judgmental about her new roommate. She'd practically jumped down his throat. There was no doubt in Isabella's mind that Danny could have been a bit more tactful, but the more she thought about it, the more she realized the point he was trying to make was valid. So what if Lisa was copying her wardrobe? *It's not the end of the world,* Isabella told herself as she walked by the campus travel agency. *Lisa's not being malicious—she just doesn't know any better.*

Standing in front of the glass windows of the bookstore, a feeling of regret surged within Isabella. She had been so absorbed in her own concerns that she had hardly addressed Danny's feelings about Josh. Not even once had she stopped to reassure Danny that he was the only one for her. Isabella couldn't wait to see Danny so she could make it up to him.

Just as she was about to walk into the bookstore, Isabella caught a glimpse of something out of the corner of her eye. It was her reflection in the window. Or at least that was what she thought at first—until she realized it was the back of her head.

That's weird, Isabella thought, doing a mental

double take. Distractedly she touched the back of her head, feeling the jagged scissor lines of her disastrous haircut and comparing them with the irregular hairline of the woman in the store. It was ironic—her hair was even the same shade of glossy black as Isabella's. Isabella stood, mesmerized by the figure walking between the book aisles, marveling at how the woman's clothes and walk were so similar to her own. *She could be my twin.*

Suddenly the woman turned around and looked in the opposite direction, giving Isabella a full view of her face.

It was Lisa.

Isabella gasped in horror, a cold chill running down her spine. *What is she doing?* She backed away from the window, moving out of Lisa's line of view. As much as she wanted to believe that Lisa had no ulterior motive, a feeling deep down inside Isabella screamed that something was terribly wrong.

"I've got to talk to someone," Isabella muttered, shoving her way through the crowd of students into the cool morning air. If she went to see Danny, he might not understand. Isabella had the sneaking suspicion that he'd only think she was overreacting again. She couldn't risk another argument with him.

The only other person she could trust— someone who would definitely understand what she was going through—was Jessica. Without hesitation Isabella cut across the quad and followed the diagonal path that ran behind the library. She walked at twice her normal speed, her stack-heeled shoes tapping incessantly against the pavement. Hopping up the steps of Dickenson Hall, Isabella silently prayed that Jessica was in her room.

"I'm sorry, she's not here," Elizabeth, Jessica's twin sister, greeted Isabella at the door. With her usual graciousness Elizabeth motioned for Isabella to come inside. "You're welcome to wait for her if you want."

The corners of Isabella's mouth tensed. While Elizabeth was good company, the thought of waiting around made Isabella uncharacteristically edgy. "You wouldn't happen to know where she went, would you?"

Elizabeth sat down at her desk, textbooks scattered around her. "I'm not sure," she said slowly, as if immersed in thought. "I think she was meeting someone, but I don't know where."

Isabella tapped her foot against the floor, her hands at her sides, tucked into anxious fists. The slimmer the chance of finding Jessica was, the more urgently she needed to talk to her. "Do you remember who she was supposed to meet?" Isabella demanded. "Anything that might give me a clue?"

"It was someone I'd never heard of before," Elizabeth answered. She scratched her head thoughtfully for a moment, then suddenly a light of recognition flashed in her eyes. "Now I remember," she said, snapping her fingers. "Jessica was going to meet some girl named Lisa."

Chapter Eight

"So what do you think?" Jessica stepped into the parlor of Theta house. She spread her arms wide, wrists held delicately in the air as though she were a game show hostess and the house was the grand prize.

"It's *fabulous*," Lisa murmured. She stepped tentatively around the furniture as if it were pieces in a museum. Turning to Jessica, her pink lips parted in a smile. "Thanks for showing me around."

"It was the least I could do after the favor you did for me," Jessica said. Lisa's sleek pantsuit and new haircut met with Jessica's enthusiastic approval. Her light brown eyes had a sparkle to them and her complexion was starting to take on a pretty pink hue. Living with Isabella was apparently doing wonders for her—Lisa looked great.

A wall of framed photographs near the parlor entrance captured Lisa's attention. She strolled silently to them, manicured fingers carefully laced behind her back.

Jessica beamed proudly at the collage of shining Theta faces. "They're our past sorority presidents," she said primly. Jessica pointed to a sepia-toned photo at the top, showing a young blond woman with delicate features. "She's my mom."

Lisa's eyes widened even more. "That's so cool," she said in a hushed voice. "It must be great to be in a sorority."

Jessica shrugged nonchalantly. "It has its bad points too."

"Like what?"

"Like having way too many frat guys asking you out at once," Jessica answered with complete seriousness. "Sometimes it's absolutely *unbearable*."

The comment must have struck Lisa as extremely funny, because she doubled over and laughed with heavy, snorting gasps.

Alison Quinn, the snobbiest member of the sorority, dropped the book she was reading and looked at Lisa with a distasteful stare. "Allergies bothering you?"

Lisa shook her head and tried to pull herself together.

"I know a wonderful doctor who could

help," Alison added in a nasty tone.

Jessica's eyes narrowed. She placed her arm protectively around Lisa's shoulders. "She's perfectly fine, thank you," she answered, steering Lisa out of the room.

"I'm sorry," Lisa whispered in the hallway.

"What's there to be sorry about?" Jessica said, loud enough for Alison to hear. "She's just grouchy because she hasn't had a date in six months."

Magda suddenly walked out of the kitchen with an apple in one hand and a quilted book bag in the other. "What's up, guys?"

Jessica gave Lisa a gentle pat on the back. "Lisa, this is Magda, our president. Magda, this is my friend Lisa. I'm giving her the tour."

"It's nice to meet you," Magda said. "I like your hair."

"Thanks," Lisa answered shyly.

Magda turned to Jessica. "I know it's a stupid question, but are you going to the Zeta party tonight?"

"What? And break my perfect attendance record?"

Lisa looked down at the floor. "What's a *Zeta* party?"

"Zeta is a fraternity," Jessica explained. "And their parties are only the most fun, most fabulous campus events around."

Magda nodded. "Why don't you go, Lisa?"

"I'd love to," Lisa said in a low voice. "But I didn't get an invitation."

"You don't need an invitation," Magda said cheerfully. "*We're* inviting you."

Lisa's eyes lit up. "Really?"

Magda took a bite of apple and headed for the door. "I've got to go, but I'll see you guys at the party tonight."

As soon as Magda was gone Lisa hopped up and down excitedly like a child on Christmas morning. "I can't wait to go!" she exclaimed.

"I haven't seen Isabella in a while, so please remind her about the party," Jessica said.

"Who else is going?" Lisa asked.

Jessica bit her bottom lip, trying to remember who was planning to show up. As far as she knew, half the campus was going to be there. "I know for sure that nearly all the sisters will be there."

"Is Josh going?" Lisa asked flatly.

Jessica nodded. "He's supposed to go with me."

Lisa smiled. "I can't believe what a funny coincidence it is that he's Isabella's old love," she said with an ironic laugh. "Isabella's hardly talked about anything else since they ran into each other."

Jessica's teeth bit deeply into her lower lip. "Is that so?"

*   *   *

Dusk was falling, the last of the sun's orange glow skimming the treetops, just as Isabella finally returned to her apartment. In between classes she'd spent the day alone, walking around campus and studying quietly in the library. Unable to find Jessica, Isabella had resorted to trying to figure out Lisa's motives on her own. *Why is she copying me?* No matter how Isabella rationalized it, she was angry.

Isabella opened the door to the foyer, glanced at the Out of Order sign that was still taped to the elevator door, and headed for the stairs. She had the entire scenario mapped out in her head. *Lisa will be in the kitchen, cleaning up or sitting on the couch, reading. I'll walk in and put my bag down without even looking at her.* Anger seared Isabella's insides as she remembered watching Lisa in the bookstore window. *If she asks me what I think about her new haircut, I'll act like it's no big deal. I won't even acknowledge that she looks just like me.* The more she thought about it, the more it made sense to Isabella not to show any reaction at all.

Finally Isabella reached the fifth floor, her heart pounding from exercise and anticipation. She took a deep breath and turned the key in the lock, fixing her face into a stony expression.

"Look who's here!" Lisa's voice chirped as

soon as the door opened a crack. Opening the door further revealed that Lisa wasn't alone. Danny was sitting at the kitchen table while Lisa poured him a cup of coffee.

Isabella's hardened expression crumbled, mixed emotions scattering across her face. Her nerves were raw with irritation as she watched Lisa scurrying around Danny in her silver slip dress and high heels, playing house. "What are you guys doing?"

Danny smiled at Lisa, and she giggled, as though they shared some secret joke. "I came over to talk to you, but you weren't here." He pointed to his mug. "Lisa offered me some coffee, so I decided to stay."

"He's on his fourth cup," Lisa said sheepishly.

Danny grinned. "I'm wired like a circuit."

Lisa broke out into uncontrollable laughter.

Any desire Isabella had earlier to make up with Danny was quickly fading. His reason for not wanting to marry her was becoming painfully obvious—he wanted to play the field. Isabella took off her coat without saying a word, allowing the heaviness of her disgust to permeate the air.

The smile instantly faded from Danny's face, but Lisa seemed completely unaware of the situation. She bobbed childishly in her chair. "You didn't say anything about my new haircut," Lisa said, touching the top of her head. "What do you think?"

Isabella threw her coat over the back of a chair. A delicious meanness streaked through her. "I think it looks like you stuck your head in a Cuisinart."

"Isabella!" Danny shouted.

Lisa was stunned. She looked as though she'd just been hit in the face with a bucket of cold water.

Isabella shrugged, smiling inwardly. "What?" she said with mock innocence. "She asked me what I thought."

"I wanted to surprise you," Lisa mumbled. Her frame drooped and her arms folded awkwardly, as if she were trying to crawl inside herself. "I thought you'd love it—now we look like sisters."

Danny glared at Isabella, his dark eyes both vexed and disappointed.

Isabella turned away from his heavy stare and opened the cupboard for a coffee mug. The shelf was empty.

"Where are all the mugs?" Isabella asked with forced lightness.

Lisa pouted her lower lip like a scolded child. "They're in the dishwasher."

"It's fixed?"

"Lisa fixed it this afternoon," Danny said intensely. "She worked on it most of the day."

Isabella paused, her back to both of them, hands gripping the counter for support. Lisa's high heels clip-clopped sullenly across the linoleum floor to the coatrack. Shame burned Isabella's cheeks.

What's wrong with me? Isabella thought. "Where are you going, Lisa?" she suddenly asked, turning around. "Danny and I are going out for a bite to eat. Don't you want to come?"

"No, thanks," Lisa answered coolly. "I have to baby-sit for Jessica again."

In a silver slip dress and heels? Isabella eyed her strangely. "Babies can be pretty messy. Don't you think you should change into something a little more casual?"

"This is fine," Lisa mumbled. Throwing a brand-new shawl over her shoulders, she looked right past Isabella. "Good night, Danny."

"Good night," he answered, waving. The moment the door closed, Danny turned to Isabella, eyes smoldering. "What's gotten into you, Isabella?" he shouted, smacking his open hand on the table. "Why do you treat her like that after everything she's done for you?"

Isabella's head swam in confusion. She didn't know whether to be embarrassed or angry. "There are two sides to every story," she said in a meek voice.

Danny rubbed his forehead tiredly. "Then

please tell me your side, because I can't figure it out at all."

Looking at his weary face, Isabella softened. Her fingers reached for the diamond ring he had given her that was hanging on the chain around her neck. *What's happening to us?* she wondered silently. They usually got along so well—they rarely argued about anything. But now every conversation seemed to deteriorate into a battle of wills.

"Try to see it from my point of view," Isabella said gently, taking a seat beside him. "I know that Lisa has done a lot for me. She's fixed all kinds of things around the apartment—and believe me, I appreciate it. But she also does things that are, well, *strange.*"

Danny looked deep into her eyes. "Like what?"

"First she bought all the same clothes as me, then she got the same haircut. She copies everything I do." Isabella spoke earnestly, hoping to make him understand how she felt. "Sometimes I feel like she's trying to take on my identity."

Instead of being sympathetic, Danny burst out laughing. "Give the girl a break, Isabella. She looks up to you—that's all."

Isabella winced. Danny's cavalier attitude felt like needles pricking her already raw nerves. "It's more than that," she insisted, covering his hand with hers. "It's like Lisa is obsessed with me."

Danny pulled his hand away. "I think if anyone's obsessed here, it's you."

This is a lot better than baby-sitting, Lisa thought as she stepped through the doors of Xavier Hall. Latin rhythms and brass horns blared from the sound system, sending the crowd on the dance floor into a wild frenzy. Brightly colored piñatas and streamers hung from the ceiling, along with a Mexican blanket with the words *Zetas Go South of the Border!* spelled out in black felt letters. There was a festive feeling in the air. Lisa felt that just about anything could happen, and she didn't want to miss one thrilling moment.

Lisa paused by the door, transfixed by the swirling colors and the authentic Mexican costumes. *What do I do now?* she wondered silently. She'd never been to a party before and had no idea how to act. The sights and sounds teased and overwhelmed her at the same time. Part of her wanted to turn around and walk right back out the door, while another part of her wanted to become completely absorbed by the pulsating music and the heat of the dancing bodies.

Just as she was deciding what to do next, Lisa felt a hand grab her shoulder. "I'm so glad you could make it!" a friendly voice called from behind.

Lisa whirled to see Jessica standing next to her. Jessica's golden hair was piled glamorously on top of her head, with long blond tendrils framing her face. She wore a flouncy scooped-neck blouse and a full red skirt that swirled around her legs. Lisa thought Jessica looked incredible.

"Great party!" Lisa shouted above the music. She clutched the shawl self-consciously around her shoulders, instantly regretting her clothing choice.

Jessica smiled a brilliant smile that sparkled even in the dark. "Come on," she said, looping her arm through Lisa's. "Let me introduce you to a couple of people."

A hot, numbing fear smothered Lisa as she inched her way behind Jessica through the crushing crowd. *Who am I going to meet?* Lisa's breath came in shallow gasps of fear at the anticipation of being introduced to new people. *Isabella can handle any social situation, but I can't. What will I say to them?* She surveyed the room with darting eyes, noting how everyone was dressed in cheerful clothes, casually standing around in groups or dancing wildly in pairs. They all fit so perfectly together, like interlocking pieces of an exclusive puzzle. Lisa imagined herself as the odd, mysterious piece that would never fit.

The first stop on their seemingly endless journey through the crowd was directly in front of the refreshment table, where a group of tall, muscular guys in mariachi suits were standing around the punch bowl. Jessica halted in front of the cutest one, who had sandy blond hair and a dimple in his chin. He was wearing a straw sombrero and a handlebar mustache carefully drawn on his face with eyeliner.

"Hi, Jay," Jessica said, shimmying up to him. Her blouse slipped seductively off her flawlessly tanned shoulders. "I'd like you to meet my friend Lisa."

I should've never come here. In panic Lisa took refuge behind Jessica, only to find herself suddenly thrust into the limelight when Jessica pushed her forward into the group of guys. "Lisa, this is Jay Knox, president of the Zeta fraternity."

Lisa's head pounded. Her tongue felt thick and dry as it searched for something to say. Jay reached for her hand, but instead of returning the handshake, Lisa's wrist was limp and lifeless. In horror she watched her hand droop, feeling completely powerless over its control.

I'm acting like a total loser. Lisa's lower lip trembled with fright. *Everyone's going to laugh at me.*

But instead of shaking her hand, Jay brought Lisa's fingers to his lips and kissed the back of her hand lightly. "It is a pleasure to meet you, señorita," he said in a fake Mexican accent.

Lisa giggled impulsively, her fingers still tingling from his kiss. *Am I really here or is this an incredible dream?* In all the years she had spent confined in a room of gray concrete walls, dreaming of glorious parties, in her wildest fantasies Lisa couldn't have imagined something so wonderful. The dazzling lights and loud music, the dancers whirling around her made Lisa feel as if she'd been swept up in a fantastic tornado of spinning colors and rhythm. She never wanted to touch the ground again.

"I haven't seen you around before," Jay said.

Lisa, still too stunned to speak, simply stared at Jay. Jessica seemed to notice the problem because she handed Lisa a cup of red punch and spoke for her. "She just transferred from New York University."

Lisa's lips parted in a frozen smile. *Don't just stand there, say something,* a voice inside her urged. Her palms were damp with perspiration. *Imagine what Isabella would say.*

Taking a sip of punch, Lisa closed her eyes for a brief moment. She pictured her perfect roommate in her mind. *You are Isabella*, she told herself. *You can handle anything*. When she opened her eyes again, a strange sense of calm hovered over her. She was transformed. Pulling her shoulders back, Lisa scanned the room with Isabella's detached, worldly gray eyes instead of her own frightened hazel ones.

Lisa opened her mouth to speak, but instead of her usual low voice a clear, velvety sound came out. "I'm Isabella's sister"—she paused to correct herself, smiling—"roommate. I moved in about a week ago."

"Speaking of Isabella, is she coming?" Jessica said, glancing at the door.

Lisa drew herself to her full height, staring Jessica straight in the eye. "I don't think so," Lisa answered. Her fingers loosened their grip on the shawl, letting it slide gracefully down to her elbows. "She said she had to meet some-one somewhere—but she wouldn't tell me any more than that."

Jessica frowned. "I wonder what could be so important."

"Shall we move on?" Lisa suggested with an aloof gaze. "There are so many people here—I don't want to miss a thing."

Jay gave her a sly wink. "If the party gets boring, you could always come back here, señorita."

Lisa tilted back her head, letting a smooth,

throaty laugh escape. "I'll keep it in mind," she answered suggestively. Then as if on cue, Lisa spun on her heels and headed into the crowd, hips swaying as she walked.

I'm the perfect girl, she thought, chanting the words in time with each footstep. *I have perfect clothes, perfect friends. . . .*

"Did she say anything about where she went?" Jessica called, trailing behind.

Lisa twirled around, one hand on her waist, the other hanging by her side like a fashion model on the runway. "Not a thing. She was pretty mysterious about it, actually." Lisa looked around with a mischievous glimmer in her eye. "So where is Josh? Didn't you say he was going to be here tonight?"

Jessica's brow wrinkled. She looked as though she'd just remembered something very disturbing. "He said he had something to do, that he couldn't make it."

"Oh," Lisa said innocently. "Too bad—I was hoping to see Josh and Isabella here. Isn't it funny how they both didn't show up?"

"Yeah," Jessica said with a scowl. "Real funny."

Chapter Nine

"Where were you last night?" Jessica said the very same moment Isabella stepped through the door of Theta house. Her blue-green eyes were as tumultuous as the Pacific after a storm.

"I was out with Danny." Isabella stared at her curiously. "We went out to dinner. Did I miss something?"

The Theta parlor was crowded with sorority sisters gathering for their weekly meeting. There were no available spaces left on the furniture, so Isabella sat on the floor. Jessica dropped down beside her.

"Did you miss something?" Jessica mimicked. "Does the word *Zeta* mean anything to you?"

Isabella let out a long sigh. "Oh, the Zeta party—I completely forgot," she said wearily. "Danny and I had a fight last night. I guess the party was the last thing on my mind."

Jessica folded her arms across her chest. "Things aren't going well between you two?" she asked in an unusually nasty tone.

"Not really," Isabella answered grimly. Her head felt heavy—she hadn't gotten much sleep, replaying the argument over and over again in her mind. "I have so much to tell you."

Lisa's new haircut and clothes, her strange mannerisms, Danny's sudden interest in her— Isabella was dying to share it all with her best friend. But before Isabella had a chance to delve into the story, the Theta meeting was called to order.

"Quiet, please," Magda said, getting the group's attention.

A dull murmur rippled through the room as conversation came to a halt. One by one the members turned with polite attention to their leader.

Magda looked down at her notes. "First of all, I want to thank those of you who went to the Zeta party last night. We had a strong showing among our sisters. I think all who attended would agree that it was a great time. For those who didn't go, just a little reminder that it's important for our sorority to support the Zetas. Please make an effort to be there next time."

Isabella felt the weighty, disapproving gaze

of Jessica, along with that of a few other sisters, turn in her direction. *It's not my fault,* she thought defensively. Jessica, of all people, had no right to give her attitude, considering that she hadn't even called Isabella to remind her about the party like she always did. Life had been so chaotic lately, there was no way Isabella would have remembered on her own.

"The next item concerns new pledges. . . ." Magda said, referring to her notes again.

Isabella shifted restlessly in her seat. *This meeting is going to take forever,* she thought tiredly. While she usually took great interest in Theta matters, on this particular day everything seemed petty and boring. There were too many issues in Isabella's personal life that needed to be addressed. Impatience seized Isabella like a fiery itch under her skin. *I need to talk to Jessica now,* Isabella thought. *She'll understand how I feel.*

Magda continued, "As you all know, Claire Edwards has transferred to another school, so we now have an opening in the sorority. If any of you know someone you'd like to pledge, please announce their names at this time."

Alison Quinn stood up immediately, smiling smugly at everyone. "I'd like to nominate Mia Salerno." Alison enunciated each word slowly and carefully, as though she were speaking to schoolchildren. "She's a freshman with a great sense of style, and her parents own one of the most successful catering businesses in the tricounty region. She'd be a fabulous contact for our sorority."

Magda made a note. "Any other nominations?"

Out of the corner of her eye Isabella watched Jessica squirm. Alison was a troublemaker of the highest order and had tried to kick Jessica out of the sorority before. At the moment there were few Alison supporters, and as far as most people were concerned, they didn't need any more.

The room was quiet for several moments. With each second of silence that passed, Alison's self-satisfied grin grew wider. It seemed as though her candidate was a shoo-in.

Then suddenly Jessica jumped to her feet. "I have someone I'd like to nominate," she said resolutely.

Good for you, Jessica, Isabella cheered silently. *Don't let Alison get away with it.* Then curiosity gripped her. Who was Jessica going to pledge?

"The person I'd like to nominate is a new student," Jessica began, looking around the room. "While she's not as polished as Alison's candidate, she's a very nice person, and I think she'd make a great contribution to our group. Her name is Lisa Fontaine."

Isabella's face fell. *Did I hear her right?* The looks she was getting from the other sisters confirmed Isabella's worst fear. *Why on earth would Jessica nominate Lisa?*

Jessica sat down, smiling at Isabella as if the nomination was supposed to make her happy. "Lisa's going to be totally psyched," she said.

"Why did you do that?" Isabella whispered.

Jessica was taken aback. "Lisa liked the house, and she said she'd love to be in a sorority."

"You showed her the house?" Isabella said aloud. A few people nearby glared at her.

"She did some baby-sitting for me, so I showed her around the house," Jessica explained quietly. "Besides, I thought you and Lisa were best buddies—I thought you'd be happy."

"Not exactly," Isabella whispered. "A lot has happened since the last time I saw you." A memory resurfaced, when Isabella had been looking for Jessica all over campus the other day. Elizabeth had mentioned that she thought Jessica had gone off to meet someone named Lisa. A fierce chill went through Isabella. First Lisa was copying her haircut and clothes, and now she was stealing her friends.

The meeting resumed. "If there are no more nominations, I'd like to move on to the next item on the agenda," Magda said. "We'll take a vote on this at the next meeting, and in the meantime I ask that you take the time to meet with the candidates personally so that you can make an informed decision."

Isabella spent the rest of the meeting in a daze, totally unaware of what was being discussed. The need to tell Jessica about the odd things Lisa had been doing smoldered inside her like hot coals. Isabella had the sneaking suspicion that Lisa was telling lies about her, which would probably explain Jessica's weird mood. But what could she possibly be saying? Regardless of what it was, Jessica needed to hear Isabella's side of things.

As soon as the meeting was over, Isabella practically pounced on Jessica. "We really need to talk," she said earnestly. "But there are too many people here—can we go to the coffee-house?"

"I don't have time," Jessica snarled. "I have to meet *my* boyfriend."

What's that supposed to mean? Isabella met Jessica's cold stare. "Look, Jess, whatever Lisa's been telling you about me, I just want you to know that there's more to this than you realize."

"This has nothing to do with Lisa," Jessica answered snidely. "And if you don't know why I'm upset, then I guess we're not as close as I thought."

* * *

She has a lot of nerve, Jessica fumed as she slammed the door to Theta house. She looked over her shoulder to make sure Isabella wasn't following her. Jessica walked down the path toward the library, book bag tightly clenched in her fist.

It was a gutsy move on Isabella's part to pretend that she'd forgotten about the Zeta party, especially when Jessica knew for a fact that Lisa had reminded her. Then Isabella claimed she spent the evening arguing with Danny. Jessica wasn't so sure she believed that one either. It was more likely that she'd met up with Josh, whose own whereabouts still hadn't been accounted for.

Jessica's sandaled feet pounded hard against the pavement as she walked across campus. Ever since that day when she discovered Isabella and Josh had once been in love, Jessica could hardly think of anything else. Whenever she saw Josh's face, she saw Isabella's too and wondered what it was like when they had been together.

Isabella's acting weird, Jessica thought. *I bet she wants him back.* Usually so sure of herself, Isabella had seemed insecure, unsteady, and preoccupied. Like that whole deal about Lisa—why would Isabella be threatened by Lisa joining the Thetas? Jessica knew Isabella well enough to realize that some major upheaval was taking place in her life, and it didn't take a rocket scientist to figure out what was causing the turmoil. It was Josh.

"Jessica!" a deep voice called from behind her.

Go away, Josh, Jessica thought, her heart aching silently. At that moment the last thing she needed was to see his gorgeous face.

"Jessica!" Josh called again.

Instinct betrayed her, and without thinking, Jessica spun on her heels and faced him. Josh moved toward her, looking sexier than ever in tight blue jeans, his thick blond hair blowing back in the breeze.

"I've been looking everywhere for you," he said, catching up to her. "Where have you been?"

"With Isabella," Jessica said dryly. "And I'm sure you knew where that was."

Josh's smoky blue eyes looked at her quizzically. "Why would I know that?"

Jessica didn't answer as she continued toward the library, eyes facing forward. "Why weren't you at the party last night?" she said finally.

"I had a project to work on for my psychology class," he answered, reaching for her hand. "But you already knew that."

"You told me you'd be at the party after you were done," Jessica countered.

Josh exhaled loudly. "I told you I'd be there if I could," he corrected. "Things took a little longer than I expected. I'm sorry." He stopped in the middle of the path, blocking Jessica's way, and reached into his backpack. "I brought you a little something to make it up to you."

Jessica tapped her toe and folded her arms in front of her. *This better be good,* she thought.

Josh looked at her nervously as he handed her a small paper bag. Jessica stared down at the object skeptically. "Go ahead," he said. "Open it."

With a violent rip Jessica tore the bag in half. She gasped as she discovered a tiny porcelain box inside that fit perfectly in the palm of her hand. It was covered in a white glaze, with a delicate ring of hand-painted flowers decorating the cover.

"Josh . . . ," she said in a hushed voice. The bitterness she had been feeling dissolved and was replaced with gratitude and love. "It's so pretty."

"They were having a sale at the student union," he said, looking pleased. "It was so beautiful, it reminded me of you."

Jessica threw her arms around Josh's neck and kissed him passionately. It was one of the nicest gifts anyone had ever given her. She had been totally wrong about him. There was no way that a guy who would do something so sweet could be capable of having an affair with her best friend.

"I'm glad you like it," Josh said, caressing her cheek with the tips of his fingers. "I'm happy with the way things are going between us, Jessica. I wouldn't do anything to wreck it."

"I know," she answered, pushing the last lingering doubt out of her mind. "I know you wouldn't."

Danny squinted at his notebook, trying to make the words sink in, but he was too preoccupied to study for tomorrow's economics exam. All he could think about was Isabella's sudden change in behavior since Josh had come into their lives.

Danny turned away from his books and looked up at his roommate. Tom Watts was trying to cram a pile of videotapes and books into his suitcase. His bus was leaving in less than two hours. "Do you plan on taking any clothes with you? After all, you'll be gone for a few days."

"Clothes . . ." Tom scratched his head, surveying the dimensions of his suitcase. "I guess not—there's no room. Besides, it doesn't matter. I'm going to a journalism conference, not a fashion show."

Danny wrinkled his nose. "I'd hate to be there on the third day, surrounded by two hundred grungy journalists. Does the convention center have windows?"

Tom picked up his suitcase and turned it upside down, spilling the contents onto his bed. "All right, *Mom*, I'll bring some clean clothes." He pulled out the top drawer of his dresser. "I thought you're supposed to be studying for your big test tomorrow."

Leaning back in his chair, Danny sighed. "I have too many things on my mind to concentrate."

"Like what I should wear to the conference?"

Danny didn't laugh. He fell silent for a moment, thinking about Isabella and her sudden change in personality. "Tom, when you went out with Jessica and her new boyfriend, what did you think of him?"

"Josh? He seemed like a great guy," Tom answered.

Danny's brow furrowed. "How great?"

Tom folded a striped rugby shirt and put it in the bottom of his suitcase. "You know— nice, funny, a good conversationalist. He's into journalism, which is cool, of course." He put in a pair of jeans and three pairs of socks. "Why are you so concerned about Jessica's boyfriend?"

Pressure started building around Danny's chest, as if someone had put an iron belt around his rib cage and was slowly pulling it tighter. From the sound of things, Josh was tough competition.

"I just found out that Josh was Isabella's high-school sweetheart."

"No way!" Tom stopped packing, his eyes practically bursting from their sockets. "That's unbelievable."

"Unfortunately it's true." Danny's lips were drawn into a thin line. "Isabella's been acting weird ever since he got here."

"You don't think—"

"I don't know what to think," Danny said grimly. "But I'm pretty sure that part of this is my fault. I know she was disappointed when I told her that the ring was just a birthday present and not a proposal."

Tom piled as many tapes as he could fit into the suitcase and zipped it closed. "Well, you could always change your mind and propose to her."

Danny rested his head against the back of the chair. "You know, I honestly thought of doing that. But it would be for the wrong reasons. Besides, now that she's so hung up on Josh, I'm starting to realize that I made the right decision after all. I don't want to be married to someone who's not committed to our relationship. I don't even know if I want to go out with someone like that."

143

"Are you saying you want to break up with her?" Tom asked.

The pressure tightened in Danny's chest until he could hardly breathe. "The way I feel right now, anything is possible."

Isabella moved through the crowd in the parlor of Theta house and headed for the kitchen to escape the sisters' probing questions about her new roommate.

"Is she as nice as Jessica says she is?" someone asked.

"Where is she from?" asked another.

"Why did Jessica nominate her? Shouldn't you be doing that?"

Isabella dodged the questions like bullets on a battlefield, smiling graciously even though she felt like dying inside. When she finally made it into the relative safety of the kitchen, she poured herself a glass of cold water.

"It looks like Lisa is the most popular candidate," she heard someone say.

This is a nightmare, Isabella thought, feeling the soothing coolness of the water on her hot, dry throat. It was bad enough to have Lisa at home, imitating everything she did. The last thing she wanted was to have her at the sorority house too.

Isabella slumped against the refrigerator, listening to the clamor of voices in the parlor.

Resentment toward Lisa was boiling to the surface. It was to the point where Isabella felt as though she could explode at any given moment. She needed an outlet. Isabella had expected Jessica to listen, but instead she'd turned on her without explanation. *If you don't know why I'm upset, then I guess we're not as close as I thought,* Jessica had snapped. What on earth was she talking about?

There was a gaping hole inside Isabella that urgently needed to be filled. She picked up the phone and dialed Danny's number. "Hi, Danny. It's me."

"What is it, Isabella?" Danny's tone was gruff, unlike his usually sensitive manner.

"I was wondering if you wanted to get together this afternoon," she said. *I'm lonely,* was what she really wanted to say.

There was a pause at the other end of the line. "Is something wrong?" he asked, his voice softening.

Finally, she thought gratefully, *someone who'll listen.* "Jessica nominated Lisa for the sorority, and when I told her I thought it was a bad idea, she went nuts on me. I wanted to go for coffee and talk about it, but she said she had other plans."

"Is that all?" he asked. "I thought something terrible had happened."

Isabella felt a hard lump forming in her

throat. The tension between them was starting all over again. "It's pretty terrible to me."

Danny let out a frustrated grunt. "Why are you bothering me over something so petty? I'm too busy for every little crisis. I have a huge test tomorrow."

"Danny, I need to talk to someone," Isabella pleaded. "I know it sounds strange, but I think Lisa's trying to turn all my friends against me."

"When are you going to realize that the world doesn't revolve around you?" he said bitingly. "Lisa's trying to get her life together, and all you can think about is how it affects you."

A tear rolled down Isabella's cheek. "It does affect me!" Panic sounded in her voice.

"I can't talk to you tonight—it'll have to wait until tomorrow," he said without emotion. "Meet me tomorrow for lunch at our favorite table in the coffeehouse."

"Danny—I need you!" she said with a strangled cry.

"What you need is some serious help," Danny said sadly. "I'm afraid I don't even know who you are anymore."

Chapter Ten

"How was your day?" Lisa chirped when Isabella came through the door. She'd just finished washing the dishes and vacuuming the living room.

Isabella didn't say a word. Puffy circles darkened her eyes. She took her coat off slowly, as if her muscles were sore. Rosie curled around Isabella's leg and meowed softly.

"I painted my nails today," Lisa said, holding up a hand for inspection. They were finally starting to grow beyond her fingertips. "They're red just like yours."

Isabella didn't answer.

Lisa's brow furrowed with concern. "Are you sick?"

Once again there was no answer. Isabella's face was stony, expressionless, her eyes glazed as though she were looking right through Lisa.

She picked up the kitten and held her carefully in her arms. "I'm going to my room," she answered numbly. "Don't bother me."

Lisa's smile turned into a frown. "You are sick, aren't you? Let me get you some aspirin."

"I don't need any aspirin." Isabella picked up the kitten and headed for her bedroom.

"Don't even think about skipping dinner. You need your strength," Lisa said in a mothering tone.

Isabella disappeared into her room, slamming the door behind her. Undaunted by her bad mood, Lisa knocked softly on the door. "Just rest," she said soothingly. "I'll make you something to eat."

Shuffling back to the kitchen in her riding boots, riding pants, and blazer, Lisa was glad to have the opportunity to help Isabella. *What's good for an upset stomach?* She searched through the cabinets, humming tunelessly to herself. The shelves were nearly bare except for a loaf of bread and a jar of jam. Lisa toasted a few slices of bread and made a cup of peppermint tea, setting the meal carefully on a wooden tray. Next to the plate she placed a few aspirins and a water glass with a flower in it, snatched from the bouquet on the table. Lisa carried the tray to the door proudly, hoping her small effort would make Isabella feel better.

Balancing the tray on one hand, Lisa knocked on the door with the other. "I'm leaving your dinner outside the door," she called. "Don't wait too long or the tea will get cold."

Lisa retreated to the couch, eyes glued to Isabella's door, waiting for her to come out. She anxiously watched to see the look of gratitude on Isabella's face, but as time ticked on, the door remained closed. There was no sign that Isabella had any intention of opening the door.

What is she doing in there? Lisa pressed her ear against the door, but no sounds came from the other side. She pounded on it, her curiosity intensifying with each knock. "Isabella? Are you all right?"

Panic suddenly hit Lisa like a freight train. *What if something's happened to her? What if she's dead?* Her insides churned in anguish. She couldn't go through something like that. Not again.

Lisa tried the doorknob, but it was locked. She slammed her shoulder against the door, but it didn't budge. "Open up!" she shouted, giving it another shove.

Lisa started to cry. Big, fat tears streaked her face. "What am I going to do?" she murmured to herself. *I won't let anything happen to you, Isabella.*

Then in a flash it came to her: the bathroom.

Dashing off to her own bedroom, Lisa plowed through, entering the bathroom from her side. There was no lock on the bathroom doors—nothing Isabella could do to keep her out.

The door creaked open, and Lisa stepped into the room. The lights were off and the curtains drawn. The room was lit only by the alarm clock on Isabella's nightstand. The numbers glowed a deep blood red, bright enough to illuminate Isabella's sleeping face.

Lisa stood next to the bed. In the dark, red light Isabella looked beautiful and peaceful, like a tranquil vampire asleep in her coffin. Lisa reached down very carefully and stroked the top of Isabella's head. With a steady hand she pulled away and touched her own hair. *I wonder if I look like that when I'm sleeping?* she thought.

Lisa bit her bottom lip deeply until she felt the sting of her teeth cutting through. An intense wave of love swelled inside her. *We're sisters now,* she thought serenely. *We're twins— nothing can come between us.*

Moving away from the bed, Lisa stood in front of Isabella's dresser. It was too dark to see, but Lisa, her hands locating each item by memory, didn't need the light.

We share everything. Nothing will come between us. Lisa's deft fingers opened the top of

Isabella's jewelry box. They grazed the cool, smooth, expensive pieces of jewelry until she found the exact object she was looking for—a pair of large, silver hoops. Putting them on, Lisa smiled in the dark. Just as easily as she found the earrings, Lisa located the small crystal bottle of French perfume that Isabella was so fond of. It smelled of delicate white flowers. Lisa dabbed it behind her ears and all the way down her neck. As the perfume penetrated her skin her body felt light and elegant, her movements fluid.

"Danny . . . ," Isabella cried in her sleep. She began to stir, rolling from one side of the bed to the other.

Lisa held her breath, perfume bottle poised in midair, waiting to see if she would wake up. With a deep groan Isabella pushed the covers off her body and clung to her pillow with both hands. Her features contorted and twisted as she sank angry teeth into the pillow. "Danny! Danny!" The cry wrenched from her throat. "Danny!"

Lisa set the perfume bottle back on the dresser. *So that's why she doesn't feel well,* she suddenly realized. Isabella wasn't sick at all—Danny had upset her.

Lisa sat on the edge of the bed and placed a comforting hand on Isabella's forehead. "Shhh . . . ," she soothed, gently touching

151

Isabella's face until she calmed down. "It's all right—no one's going to hurt you. I'm here."

Isabella's shouts quieted to an incomprehensible whimper. She rolled onto her side and her breathing became normal again, her body relaxed. Lisa pulled the comforter up to Isabella's chin.

I should've known Danny was behind it all. Did they break up? It was more than Lisa could hope for. It was too soon, but from the looks of things, Danny and Isabella were well on their way. From the moment she met Isabella, Lisa wanted to be just like her. The friends, the parties, the clothes, even the boyfriend—she wanted it all. She was close to getting the first three things—now the only thing left was Danny.

I'm doing you a favor, Isabella, Lisa thought. It was totally obvious that Danny was only stringing her along until something better came his way. Not only that, but Danny was too demanding of Isabella's time. Every moment she spent with him was time that she should have been spending with Lisa. It had to stop.

Spotting Isabella's trench coat folded over the back of her desk chair, Lisa picked it up and put it on. "Don't worry about a thing, sweet sister," she whispered into the darkness. "No one will ever come between us again."

＊ ＊ ＊

Danny woke with a start. His eyes opened anxiously to the darkness, his heart pounding. *Someone's in my room,* he thought with alarm. Propping himself up on his elbows, he listened intently. It was quiet. The alarm clock next to his bed read 12:30. *You were dreaming, Wyatt,* he told himself as he rolled over and pulled the sheet up to his neck. *You're too stressed out about your test tomorrow. Relax.*

The beating of Danny's heart slowed to a normal pace and his breathing became even again as the sweet heaviness of sleep returned to him. Just as he began to tumble into another dream, he woke again suddenly. *I'm not imagining it,* he thought breathlessly. *Someone or something is definitely in my room.*

"Who's there?" he whispered hoarsely. There was no answer.

Danny sat up again and blinked a few times as his eyes adjusted to the darkness. Slowly a figure took shape before his eyes, a faint outline against the black of night. His knees trembled with fright.

"Who are you?" he shouted to the figure. It drew closer to him, gliding its way across the room as if it were floating an inch above the floor. The figure made a faint rustling sound as it moved closer. Every nerve in Danny's body was on edge, and his muscles

153

tightened, anticipating a confrontation.

The figure stood quietly over the edge of the bed, dissolving in and out of the shadows like a ghost or an apparition. Danny's terrified eyes watched in paralyzing fear while his fingers curled defensively into hard fists. Whatever was about to happen, he was ready for it.

"I'm warning you," he said in a deep voice, with much more confidence than he felt. "You'd better leave me alone."

The figure hovered only inches above his face, letting out a low giggle. It was a woman's voice. Danny's fists immediately relaxed, his head feeling disoriented and confused.

Now I really must be dreaming, he thought.

Danny fumbled for the light switch, but the figure's slender hand grabbed his wrist and pulled it away. Her fingers were warm and solid—not at all like a ghost or a dream. Danny swallowed hard. She was real.

"Maybe you should tell me what you're doing here," he said, his bravado mellowing into a husky, pleading tone.

She giggled again but didn't answer him. Releasing her grip of his wrist, she leaned over and pressed her cheek against his. The familiar scent of French perfume sent an exhilarating shiver through the length of his body. Her lips traced a path across his cheek to his ear, softly nibbled at his earlobe, then worked their way down his neck.

"It's you . . . ," Danny breathed with relief as his fingers grazed the familiar cloth of Isabella's trench coat. His hands reached up and touched her closely cropped hair. "Why didn't you say something?"

She answered him with a trail of fiery kisses burning across his collarbone, concentrating on the soft spot in the hollow of his neck.

Danny closed his eyes with pleasure. "I'm sorry I haven't been more understanding recently," he hummed. "I miss the way things used to be between us."

He lifted his head and drew her up toward him. She reached for his mouth hungrily with her passionate kiss. Danny's breathing came in short, heavy gasps.

Isabella's never acted like this before, he thought as the kiss deepened. As thrilling as the interlude was, something seemed to be missing. The intensity was there, but the romance, the tenderness was gone. It felt almost desperate.

"Oh, Isabella," he murmured, pulling away from her to catch his breath. She didn't stop for a moment, her busy hands sliding down the collar of his pajama top, at last finding the buttons.

Overwhelmed by the sudden change in

Isabella, Danny froze as she undid the top two buttons. His body burned with desire, but sirens were blasting in his head, warning him that things were going way too far. Her hands teased him like searing flames.

"No . . . ," he said, gathering his resolve. "We can't do this."

She paused for a second, then continued to undo to the third button as if she didn't hear him. Isabella had never been so out of control before.

Danny raged against his senses. "I mean it," he said, louder this time. "I love you, but we can't do this."

She yanked away from him suddenly, leaving the third button of his pajamas intact. Danny half expected her to shout curses at him, but no sound came from her. Her actions said it all.

"Look," he said apologetically. "I'm so glad that you're not upset with me, but you don't have to come here in the middle of the night to prove it."

She sat quietly in the darkness, not saying anything. Danny ran his fingers through her hair. "Instead of meeting for lunch like we planned, let's meet for breakfast instead. I can't wait to see you."

She reached over and kissed him again. Then silently she disappeared into the black of night.

The next morning Lisa hid behind the fake plastic palm trees in the coffeehouse, watching Danny from a distance. He was sitting at a cozy table for two by the window, reading a newspaper. The morning sun cast a golden light on his strong shoulders and neck. Lisa glowed as she studied his full, soft lips, remembering their encounter in his room the night before. The memory of it sent a delicious shiver through her. She'd never been kissed like that before.

And he played the game so perfectly, she thought. The whole time he pretended it was Isabella he was kissing when he had to have known it was Lisa instead. *He wants me just as much as I want him.*

The fact that Danny responded so easily to Lisa's touch confirmed in her mind that he no longer wanted to be with Isabella. But Danny was too much of a coward to break up with her. Instead he tried to pretend that nothing was wrong, even though Isabella could sense that things weren't right. He was making her miserable. Danny was obviously ready to move on to a new, more exciting relationship. All Lisa had to do was give him a nudge in the right direction.

Lisa smoothed down her hair and brushed the wrinkles out of her miniskirt. *Isabella won't mind—she has Josh.* Lisa sighed contentedly, imagining all the double dates they could go on together. There was no doubt in her mind—this was the perfect plan.

Danny glanced down at his watch, his face creased with worry lines.

You've waited long enough, my love. Lisa stepped out from behind the palm trees and strode over to the table. She casually slid onto the stool across from his and flashed him a look of sympathy. "You look like you've been stood up."

"I have been." Danny glowered. He didn't look as happy to see her as she'd expected. "Isabella was supposed to be here half an hour ago. Is she still at the apartment? Maybe she overslept."

Lisa shook her head. "Isabella left the apartment hours ago," she said with a lilt to her voice. "I have no idea why she's not here or where she went. She's so hard to keep track of."

Danny frowned, looking down at his coffee cup.

You can stop playing the game anytime now, Danny, Lisa thought with exasperation. *A man your age should know when to quit.* Then there was always the chance that he was in denial. Any good boyfriend would be able to tell the difference between his girlfriend and an impostor. Lisa was sure that Danny knew it

158

wasn't Isabella he was kissing last night.

"What are you having for breakfast?" Lisa asked cheerfully, peering over his plate. Lisa flagged down the waitress, who came running over without hesitating. Lisa smiled to herself. "I'll have what he's having."

Danny seemed dazed, his eyes focused on some faraway place. "Decaf and an almond croissant," he answered flatly.

"Sounds good." Lisa giggled.

Danny drank solemnly from his cup as if Lisa weren't even there. His sullenness sparked a flash of white-hot anger inside Lisa. *You're not going to sit there and sulk about her, are you?* she raged silently. *I'm the one you want, Danny. Not Isabella.*

"I just don't get it," Danny said aloud. He looked up, but his gaze seemed to travel right through Lisa. "She's been acting so strange lately."

The silver chain Lisa had bought yesterday felt cool against her skin. Tonight she planned to go shopping for a ring to hang from it. She leaned toward Danny. "Just between you and me, I don't think Isabella has ever had her priorities straight," she whispered in a confidential tone. "If I had a boyfriend, I'd make sure he came first. I wouldn't take him for granted."

Danny's brows knitted. "Isabella's not a bad

159

girlfriend—she's just preoccupied. Something's going on in that head of hers. I just can't figure it out."

Lisa tilted her head coyly to the side. "Poor Danny," she said in a velvet voice, despite the fact that her patience was wearing very thin. "You just don't get it, do you?"

Snapping out of his daze, a look of fright lit Danny's dark eyes. "What do you mean?"

"Your heart's too big to see what's really going on here," Lisa answered. The waitress returned, setting the breakfast in front of her. Lisa picked up the coffee cup and took a delicate sip before continuing. "I've seen this before with friends of mine. I hate to say it, but I think Isabella's giving you the brush-off because she wants you to break up with her."

Danny shook his head adamantly. "I thought so too for a while, but something happened yesterday to change my mind. Isabella and I both know that we're terrific together, and we can work through anything. There's no reason in the world for us to break up."

"Maybe none that you know of." Lisa gritted her teeth. Why was Danny working so hard to deny the truth? "You deserve better, Danny."

Standing up, Danny folded his newspaper into quarters and drained the last of his coffee. "Thanks for the advice, but I think your theory is way off. Isabella and I may have had a temporary setback, but as soon as we talk it out we'll go back to having a normal life together."

Don't bet on it, Lisa thought stubbornly as she watched him walk away. She ate a bit of croissant, thinking of how wonderful things were going to be when he finally realized that it was over between him and Isabella. *You just wait, Danny Wyatt*, Lisa vowed silently as he walked out the door. *I'll make you forget that Isabella Ricci ever existed.*

Chapter Eleven

Where is he? Isabella checked her watch again, each time her heart sinking a little deeper. Over and over again she replayed in her mind the conversation they'd had the day before when she'd called Danny from Theta house, begging to see him. Danny had been cold and uncaring, saying he couldn't see her until lunch the next day. Maybe he didn't want to see her, but Danny wasn't the kind of person to break a promise. He had to show up.

Maybe he's running late, Isabella thought with a glimmer of hope. She decided to stick around for at least another twenty minutes or so just to be sure. Besides, there was nowhere else to go. There was no one else to talk to.

Thoughtfully Isabella circled the rim of the coffee cup with one short, unpolished fingernail. The sight of Lisa's new manicure had sent

Isabella into a rage last night. In a fury she'd clipped her beautifully groomed long finger-nails right down to the fingertips and removed every trace of red polish. She refused to be Lisa's twin and would fight her every step of the way.

To the average person, Isabella imagined that her anger over what Lisa had been doing would probably seem unreasonable. But it wasn't. *All I need is five minutes,* she thought. *If Danny will just listen to me for five minutes, he'll understand what I'm going through.* Tension pulled at every fiber of her when she thought of how Lisa had managed to imitate every aspect of her personality. Isabella was tense every moment Lisa was in the apartment. Seeing Lisa was like staring into some creepy fun-house mirror. It was like looking at some eerie, distorted view of herself.

The door to the coffeehouse swung open, and Isabella looked up, anticipating Danny's handsome face. But it wasn't him. Isabella's hopes were crushed once again. "Don't do this to me, Danny," she whispered under her breath. "Don't abandon me when I need you the most."

Danny had always been there when she needed him—until now. An icy chill flowed through her veins. *Is this the end, Danny?* Isabella wondered, tears welling up in her eyes. *Is it over between us?*

163

Lisa strutted down the corridor of the English department, silver bangles jingling from her delicate wrist as she walked. Jay Knox and a few other guys in Zeta jackets were sitting on one of the benches outside Professor Connor's office. Lisa held her head high as she swayed past, feeling their heavy stares.

"Good afternoon, señorita," Jay said.

Lisa turned her head slowly, giving the group a seductive crimson smile. Then, without saying a word, she continued toward her intended target at the end of the hall.

"You should come visit me sometime," Jay called behind her. "I have a nice piñata I'd like to show you." The group broke out into hysterics.

Lisa ignored the comments, her mind focused only on the tall, gorgeous blond at the end of the hall. Josh was leaning against the wall outside his adviser's office, writing in his notebook.

"Hey, Josh," Lisa said, tapping lightly on his shoulder.

Josh looked up from his writing. "Hi, Lisa. What's up?"

Lisa pouted her lips and ran her fingers through her hair. "I came to see my adviser, Dr. Kelly."

"Kelly's your adviser too?"

Lisa nodded. "I've decided to major in English."

"Good choice," Josh answered, his smoky blue eyes shining. "Kelly's a great adviser."

"That's good to know." Lisa leaned against the wall beside him and glanced at his notebook. "Getting caught up on some letters?"

Josh's soft lips twitched thoughtfully. "Actually I'm writing a letter to Jessica."

A curious expression came over her face. "Do you guys often communicate by mail?" She giggled playfully.

"Not exactly," Josh said. "I have to cancel our weekend plans to go to Malibu—something came up. I know Jess is going to be disappointed, and I don't want to be around when the volcano erupts."

Lisa nodded knowingly. "How are you breaking it to her?"

"As gently as possible." He turned the notebook toward her. "Here—tell me what you think."

Leaning closer to him, Lisa pretended to read the note, conscious only of Josh's body. She lowered her head, feeling her short hair brush against his shoulder. Squinting, she pretended to study the note carefully, holding out for as long as she could. "It looks fine to me," she said finally. "After all, you *are* an English major."

Josh smiled and ripped the letter out of his notebook. "I've got to go put this letter in Jessica's mailbox, so if you'll excuse me . . ."

Lisa squeezed his elbow, holding him back. "I'm going over to the student union right now," she said. "I could do it for you."

"I thought you were here to see Dr. Kelly."

"I *am*, but I just remembered that I left the paper he was supposed to sign back in my room." She touched her silver earring self-consciously. "I'm sure you've got a lot to do. I wouldn't mind helping out at all."

Josh rubbed his strong jaw. "Actually Elizabeth is expecting me at WSVU right about now," he said, thinking aloud. "As long as you don't mind. It's really important, so make sure it gets in her mailbox."

"I promise," Lisa said, smiling brilliantly. She tucked the note into her leather handbag. Suddenly her face grew serious. "You know, I was walking by the coffeehouse a few minutes ago and I saw Isabella sitting in the window. She was all by herself and she looked terrible." She spoke in a grave tone. "To tell you the truth, I'm a little worried about her. She hasn't been herself lately."

Tiny worry lines formed around Josh's eyes. "What's wrong?"

"I really don't know," Lisa said heavily. "She won't talk to me, or anyone for that matter.

She's practically shut Danny out of her life completely."

Josh swallowed hard. "Do you think it's serious?"

Lisa shrugged. "It's hard to tell. I am a little nervous about leaving her by herself, but what can I do? I can't spend the whole day watching over her. I don't *think* she'll do anything drastic . . ."

With a determined look Josh grabbed his jean jacket. "Thanks for telling me. I'm going to head over there right now." He headed down the hall.

"What about WSVU?" Lisa called after him.

"It can wait!" Josh said before disappearing around the corner.

"I can't stand this anymore," Isabella mumbled to herself, throwing down a handful of change to pay for her coffee. Danny was officially an hour late. It was time to leave.

Reaching for her handbag, Isabella heard the footsteps of someone approaching. To her surprise, it was Josh.

"May I join you?" he said.

Isabella ran a quick finger under her eyelids to remove any traces of tears or running mascara. She smiled weakly at him. "I was just leaving."

"That's too bad," he said with frown. "I didn't want to eat lunch all alone."

"I don't blame you," Isabella answered dryly. "It's not much fun."

Josh pulled out a stool for her to sit on. "Then won't you stay out of sympathy for an old friend?"

Isabella hesitated for a moment, then sat down. She didn't want to burden Josh with her problems, but at the same time she didn't want to be alone.

Isabella felt self-conscious in her floral rayon skirt and blouse that were in desperate need of dry cleaning. She had felt emotionally drained when she woke up, and the outfit was the first thing she'd reached for. Isabella hadn't even bothered with perfume or jewelry, and the red, burning eyes she had from crying didn't help matters.

"How are things going for you?" she asked tiredly.

"I've been better," Josh answered, staring right at her. "How are things going with *you?*"

He knows something's wrong. Should I tell him about Lisa? The question turned over again and again in her brain. Even though Isabella desperately needed someone to listen to her problem, it had been years since she'd had a real talk with Josh. They'd lost touch—they hardly knew anything about each other anymore. If Jessica and Danny couldn't understand her feelings and they knew her better than anyone else, how could Josh possibly understand?

"Life has been pretty lousy lately," she said, staring down at the unlit votive candle in the middle of the table. "I'd rather not talk about it."

Josh nodded. "It's your choice, but I'm here if you need me."

Isabella smiled for what felt like the first time in days. "Thanks for saying that." She covered his hand with hers. "It means a lot to me."

"I know things sort of fell apart when we went off to college, but I never stopped caring about you." Josh placed his other hand on top of Isabella's. "You were my first love, Isabella. I will always love you."

"Lisa!" Jessica called, jogging across the quad to catch up with her. It was a perfect sunny day, and the sky was a brilliant California blue.

"You're just the person I was looking for," Lisa said, squinting into the sun. "If you don't have any lunch plans, I was hoping you'd like to eat with me."

Jessica was surprised to see that she was wearing makeup—a dusting of translucent powder on her face, a touch of mascara, and carefully painted red lips. Obviously Isabella must have been teaching Lisa her makeup secrets. She looked fabulous.

Jessica smiled. "Sounds great," she said. "Is your roommate coming too? I need to talk to her about something."

Ever since the Theta meeting Jessica had felt terrible about how she'd given Isabella the cold shoulder, especially since Josh insisted that he hadn't been spending any time alone with Isabella. Once again jealousy had gotten the best of Jessica, and she wanted to tell Isabella how sorry she was.

"I haven't seen Isabella since last night," Lisa explained, shaking her head. "She's always running off somewhere."

"That's OK—I'll catch up with her later," Jessica said. They cut across the soft green grass of the quad. "Did she tell you the good news?"

Lisa's sparkling hazel eyes narrowed. "What good news?"

The corners of Jessica's mouth turned down. "I thought she would've at least told you. You've been nominated to become a member of the Theta sorority."

A look of confusion came over Lisa's face, then slowly her features lit up with excitement as the words began to sink in. "I can't believe it!" she shouted, her voice echoing off the nearby English building. "I'm going to be in a sorority!" Lisa threw her arms around Jessica's neck.

"Not so fast," Jessica said calmly. "Right now you're only a candidate. There's one other person up for it, and in the next week or so the Thetas are going to take a vote."

Lisa gazed wistfully at the blue sky. Jessica had no idea that the nomination would mean so much to her.

"This is like a dream come true for me. I've never been so happy in my whole life. Thanks so much, Jess," she gushed. "I want to celebrate. Instead of us going to the cafeteria, let me treat you to lunch at the coffeehouse."

"You don't need to do that," Jessica said modestly.

Lisa took Jessica by the arm and steered her toward the brick building in front of the library. "I want to do it."

Jessica relented. "If you insist."

"Good." Lisa reached into her handbag and pulled out a folded piece of paper. "I ran into Josh earlier, and he asked me to give this to you."

Staring curiously at the paper, Jessica took it from her. "What does it say?"

Lisa shrugged. "I don't know—I figured it was none of my business, so I didn't read it. It's probably just a mushy love note."

They stopped at the entrance of the coffeehouse while Jessica unfolded the letter and read it silently to herself. "Oh no," she said out loud as she got to the bottom of the note. Her shoulders dropped in disappointment. "I can't believe this."

"What?" Lisa said with concern.

Jessica crumpled the letter into a ball and tossed it into a nearby trash can. "Josh is canceling our weekend plans. We were supposed to go to Malibu," she said sourly. "And he didn't even give me an explanation."

"Maybe he wants to tell you in person," Lisa said optimistically. "I'm sure he has a good reason."

Jessica's blood ran cold. "He'd better."

The door to the coffeehouse opened and a few students came out, sending a wave of jazz music into the open air. As soon as the entrance was clear Lisa walked in ahead of Jessica. Lisa had barely made it through the door when she whirled around suddenly, a look of alarm on her face.

"You can't come in!" Lisa said anxiously.

"Why not?" Jessica craned her neck to see what the big deal was.

Lisa gently nudged her backward. Her eyes shifted nervously from side to side. "Trust me, you don't want to see."

"See what?" Curiosity seized Jessica as she pushed her way through the door past Lisa.

172

Then Jessica understood perfectly. Sitting at a little romantic table for two was her boyfriend, and he wasn't alone. He was with Isabella.

Jessica's heart plunged to the floor.

"I was afraid something like this might happen," Lisa said sadly.

Hot, angry tears stung Jessica's eyes. "Me too."

Lisa wrapped a supportive arm around Jessica's shoulders. "If you want to confront them, I'll stand by you."

"No," Jessica said through gritted teeth as she backed out the door. "I don't have *anything* to say to those two backstabbers."

"Good morning!" Lisa answered the telephone in a bright, singsong voice. "Ricci residence, Lisa speaking."

The voice at the other end wasn't quite so cheery. "Where's Isabella?" Danny demanded.

Lisa's pleasant mood was slipping fast. When was he going to stop pining for Isabella? "She's not here," Lisa answered.

"I left a ton of messages on her machine yesterday, and she didn't call me back."

"I'm so sorry to hear that. . . ." Lisa flipped open the lid of the answering machine and peered down at the empty slot where the incoming message tape was supposed to be. She had removed it yesterday because of Danny's

173

persistent calls, tucking it away in her carved box for safekeeping. "Isabella still wasn't home when I went to bed last night."

There was a pause. "Is she home now?" Danny's voice wavered. "I need to talk to her, Lisa. It's important."

"Hold on one second, I'll check." She dropped the phone on the couch and tiptoed through the bathroom into Isabella's bedroom. Isabella was asleep, sprawled out on top of her bedcovers, wearing a pair of dirty jeans and an old sweatshirt. Rosie was curled up by her side.

You look like you had another rough night, Lisa thought with pity, looking at Isabella's pale, tear-stained cheeks. Despite what Lisa had told Danny, it was the second day in a row that Isabella had come home and gone straight to bed. Isabella hadn't said a word to Lisa in the last two days. *It hurts to be ignored by your own sister,* she thought. The pain was sharp and deep—almost electric. It reminded Lisa of the shock therapy they had given her in the place she had lived before. It had made her cry.

"You can't talk to him," Lisa whispered angrily at Isabella's sleeping face. "You don't deserve it."

Lisa stormed back to the phone, swallowing the rage that splintered inside her. "She's not here, Danny," she answered. "And her bed hasn't been slept in."

Danny's voice broke. "Are you sure?"

"Quite." Lisa sighed heavily. *At this rate he's never going to let go of her.* "Listen, Danny, there's something you should know, but I can't tell you over the phone." She glanced at the door to Isabella's room. "Can I come over?"

Chapter Twelve

"Are you sure this isn't all some huge misunderstanding?" Elizabeth closed the copy of
Chaucer's *Canterbury Tales* that she was reading for English class and looked up at her sister.
Jessica's purple satin pillows were stained with
tears and her face was flushed. "I'm sure there's
a perfectly good explanation, Jess."

"I know what I saw!" Jessica wailed, beating her fists on the mattress. "They were sitting alone together, holding hands. What more
proof do you need?"

"Sometimes things aren't what they seem,"
Elizabeth answered in the calm, rational tone
that drove Jessica insane. "After all, do you
really think Josh and Isabella would do something so stupid as to hold hands in a public
place?"

Jessica angrily snatched the latest issue of

Ingenue magazine off her bookshelf and opened to page fifty-two. "The proof is right here, Liz," she shouted, pointing to the article. "It's a quiz—'Rate Your Mate: How to Find Out if Your Boyfriend Is Cheating on You.'"

A smug grin played at the corners of Elizabeth's pretty mouth. "I think you've been wearing your dresses a little too tight these days, Jess. Not enough blood is getting to your brain."

Jessica's blood began to boil. "Laugh all you want—this quiz opened my eyes to a lot of things," she seethed. "For example, question one—'Does your boyfriend give you flowers for no reason?'" She stared intensely at her sister. "Liz, the other day Josh gave me a hand-painted box covered with flowers."

"Oh no! What a mean guy," Elizabeth said dryly. "I hope you told him off."

Jessica returned to the magazine with determination. "OK, then, how about this—'Does your beau cancel plans at the last minute?'" She was certain Elizabeth couldn't argue this one. "He canceled our trip to the beach this weekend—without any explanation!"

To Jessica's surprise, Elizabeth was completely unfazed. "Plans change all the time. You can't call that proof."

"That's not all," Jessica continued on. "Number three—'Does your boyfriend avoid telling you things in person?' The answer to that is a big, fat yes! He sent me a note this morning instead of breaking the news to my face."

Elizabeth's lips twitched humorously. "You'd make a lousy lawyer," she said. "Your evidence is purely circumstantial at best. If I were a judge, I'd throw your case right out of court."

Jessica scowled. "It's a good thing you're not a judge, then. I took the whole quiz, and Josh scored an eighteen out of twenty questions. According to this, he's a Runaround Randy!"

Elizabeth leaned back in her chair and laughed spastically.

"It's not funny!" Jessica shouted. "The Super Bonus section proves that he's cheating on me with my best friend!"

Elizabeth snatched the magazine out of Jessica's grasp and tossed it into the wastepaper basket. "You can't believe those stupid magazines. They only put those quizzes in there to sell more copies—they have no basis in reality," she said, handing Jessica a tissue. "Real-life situations are much more complex than such a simplistic set of questions."

"Thanks for the commentary, Einstein." Jessica blew her nose. The thought of Isabella and Josh betraying her chilled her to the core.

It reinforced her belief that you couldn't trust anyone. "It doesn't matter. I still think he's cheating on me."

Just as Elizabeth was about to hand her another tissue, there was a knock at the door. "I'll get it," Elizabeth said, bounding across the room to answer it.

"Whoever it is, tell them I'm not here," Jessica called, burying her face in her pillow. Elizabeth could make fun all she wanted, but it didn't make the situation any easier or any less painful. When Jessica found out that Isabella and Josh had dated before, a nagging fear in the back of her mind made her wonder if they'd get back together again. Josh had slyly convinced her that it wasn't true, and Jessica had blamed herself for feeling jealous. But now that her worst fears had been realized, Jessica was totally unprepared for the deep shock that racked her body and tortured her mind. The whole situation was much worse than any she could have imagined.

"I just want to talk to her—" said the familiar voice at the door. Jessica lifted her head. It was a voice she had hoped never to hear again. It was Isabella.

In a rage Jessica flew off her bed and lunged at the door. Reason escaped her temporarily, making her act on instinct alone. Elizabeth jumped out of the way as Jessica flung open the door. "What do you want?" she bellowed.

Isabella was startled, her face gaunt. "I'm sorry. If this is a bad time, I could come back later. . . ."

Jessica folded her arms across her chest and stood with her feet apart, ready for a confrontation. "This is as good a time as any," she said fiercely. "Go ahead and say what you have to say."

Looking over her shoulder, Isabella glanced at the people passing in the hallway. They were staring at the two of them, waiting to see what was going to happen next. "Maybe I should come inside," she said in a low voice.

"Whatever you have to say, you can say it out here," Jessica barked.

As if on cue, tears glistened in Isabella's eyes. "I don't know what I've done to make you so mad at me, Jess, but things are pretty rough for me right now. I really need a friend."

What an actress, Jessica thought. *How pathetic can you be to steal my boyfriend, then cry on my shoulder afterward?* Jessica clapped and cheered. "You deserve an Academy Award for that performance," she said sarcastically.

"It's Lisa, isn't it?" Isabella's jaw clenched. "I think she's been spreading lies about me."

Jessica looked at her with pity. "Go ahead, Isabella, blame everyone but yourself." Moving closer, she waved a threatening finger at her.

"But let me tell you one thing—Lisa is an honest, decent human being, which is a whole lot more than I can say for you."

"What?" Danny staggered backward and gripped his desk chair to steady himself. He looked at Lisa dizzily, as if the world were tilting on its axis and everything in his room was about to come crashing down around him. "It can't be—"

"They've been seeing each other for a week now." Lisa watched with detachment as Danny's dark eyes change from disbelief to horror to agonizing pain. *Why are you making this so hard for yourself? I thought you'd be happy now that we can be together.* How long did she have to keep playing this game?

"I'm sorry you had to find out this way," she said in a honey-soaked voice.

Danny rubbed his forehead in slow, rhythmic circles. "I suppose it's better than catching them together. I don't think I could handle that shock," he said weakly. "Does Jessica know?"

"Unfortunately, yes. We saw them together at the coffeehouse." Lisa sat down on the edge of Danny's bed and crossed her long legs. "She's devastated."

Danny's expression was dour. "So am I."

Then get over it. Lisa's patience was nearing

the breaking point. All her life she'd been waiting to have a boyfriend she could call her own, and now every minute she waited was excruciating. When would he get over Isabella?

"As I think back, Isabella's cheating on me explains a lot of things," Danny said. He turned his back to the window and gazed at the far wall. "She's been acting strange ever since Josh came back into her life."

With her arms crossed in front of her, Lisa pinched her sides until she felt her eyes watering involuntarily. "I suspected this a long time ago," she said in a weepy voice. She sniffled a little for added effect. "I should've said something to you earlier—I feel like this is all my fault."

Danny held her by her narrow shoulders. His hands were strong. "Don't blame yourself," he said firmly.

Covering her face with her hands, Lisa shook her shoulders up and down as if she were sobbing. "Like I've said before, you deserve so much better, Danny. I hate to see you hurt."

"Shhh . . ." Danny's outstretched arms pulled her closer, and Lisa pressed herself eagerly against him. He rested his head on her shoulder for comfort, each breath he took a heavy sigh. "Of all the people I have ever dated, Isabella was the last one I'd expect to do this to me."

"People will surprise you," Lisa said ruefully. She felt Danny's heart beating in time to her own. Tenderly she rubbed his muscular back, bloodred fingertips tracing the perfect line of his spine all the way up to his gorgeous neck. Her head was light, overwhelmed by the strength of the arms that enveloped her. *You'll learn to love me, Danny, I promise.*

Lisa's slitted eyes gazed blissfully out the window, down to the quad below. Several yards ahead she spotted someone walking down the path that led to the dorm. The dark hair and the graceful walk were all too familiar. *Is that who I think it is?* Lisa's eyes opened wide as the figure drew closer. She was right—it was Isabella.

This is too good to be true. Even Lisa had to admit that she couldn't have orchestrated a more perfect plan. Isabella marched on, heading right for the dorm. In a matter of seconds she would pass by the window and see Lisa in Danny's arms.

Please don't let go of me, Danny, Lisa pleaded silently. *Hold on for just another minute or so. . . .*

Despite her silent pleas, Danny let go. Lisa locked her arms firmly around him, but Danny took her by the elbows and eased her grip. "Thanks for telling me—you're a true friend," he said. "But I think I just need to be alone right now."

"No—you're wrong," she said quickly. "The worst thing in the world is for you to be alone." Isabella was only a few feet away now. Time was running out. *Think of something— fast,* a voice inside her head told her. *You're missing the perfect opportunity.*

Danny shook his head. Taking her by the hand, he pulled Lisa away from the window and out into the hallway. "Thanks for your concern, but I'll be all right."

Maybe Isabella's coming to see him. Hope surged through her. Any minute now she could be coming up the stairs and she would see them together. Lisa had to stall just in case.

With another pinch to her side, Lisa forced her eyes to tear again. "I hope so," she said in a whisper. Impulsively she laced her fingers behind Danny's neck and managed to turn him around slightly so that if Isabella came up the stairs, she would have a better view of them both. Danny's arms wrapped hesitantly around her as Lisa rested her cheek against his warm shoulder. She closed her eyes dreamily, but not before she caught a glimpse of Isabella's horrified face staring at them from the doorway near the stairwell. A slow, satisfied smile crossed Lisa's lips. Mission accomplished.

Trust me, Isabella, Lisa thought. *It's for your own good.*

* * *

I can't believe this is happening to me. Isabella's steel gray eyes were glued to the end of the hallway, where Danny and Lisa were in a tight clinch. The blood in her veins felt as if it were crystallizing and her heart was turning to ice.

It didn't surprise her that Lisa was capable of such betrayal, but not Danny. *I have to get out of here,* she thought, suddenly feeling out of breath. Seeing them together was like standing on the brink of the deep, dark, bottomless chasm of insanity. Isabella was terrified that if she looked at them a moment longer, she'd tumble into the pit and completely lose her mind.

Heavy tears poured from her eyes as she ran blindly down the stairs, out the front door, and across the quad to the outskirts of campus. She stopped by the pond and sat down on the edge of the muddy bank. The tips of her sneakers dipped into the murky water, but Isabella didn't even notice. She was too preoccupied by the pain in her heart. Every thought of Danny was a razor-sharp blade tearing at her insides. "How could he do this to me?" she sobbed out loud, head and arms resting on her knees. *How could he throw it all away for someone he hardly knows?*

In a fit of rage Isabella grabbed the ring Danny had given her for her birthday and yanked it off the chain around her neck. She clenched the cold diamond ring and the broken chain in her fist. Lifting her hand high in the air, Isabella drew back her arm, poised to throw the ring into the pond.

"Here's what I think of you, Danny Wyatt!" she shouted, her voice cracking. Isabella's arm snapped forward, but her hand wouldn't release the ring. It was a Wyatt family heirloom and meant a lot to Danny.

A fresh wave of tears hit her as she shoved the ring into the pocket of her jeans. As deeply as Danny had hurt her, Isabella still couldn't bring herself to hurt him back. Her mind cried out for revenge, but her heart rendered her powerless.

Looking out over the cool smoothness of the pond, Isabella wondered what to do next. Now that she no longer had a boyfriend or a best friend, she didn't know who else to turn to. She'd never felt so totally alone before. It was like being trapped in a fishbowl, watching the world around her but being horribly separated from it at the same time.

Isabella lowered her head sadly. In the mirrorlike stillness of the pond, she saw her reflection. *Is that really me?* she wondered, watching the wild-eyed, rumpled-looking girl staring back at her. Isabella touched her haggard face, her messy hair, the baggy sweatshirt she was wearing. The woman in the reflection was disheveled, insecure, miserable. It reminded her of Lisa, and how she had looked when she'd first moved in. Now Lisa was the one who was poised and gracious . . . . the one who had all the friends.

Suddenly everything was beginning to fit together in Isabella's mind. Despite what everyone seemed to think, Lisa's transformation was no accident.

"At least let me in so we can talk about this," Josh begged. Jessica opened the door only a few inches, just enough so he could see the smoldering look in her eyes.

"There's nothing to talk about," Jessica hissed. "Just leave."

Despite the searing anger that roiled inside her, the sight of Josh's soft blond hair and smoky eyes was dampening her resolve.

"OK, Jess, I admit it—I messed up." He leaned his towering body against the doorframe. "I should've told you in person."

"You shouldn't have done it at all!" Jessica shouted, the fire resurging. Her lower lip trembled. "You dirty double-crosser!"

Josh took a step back. "If I had known you'd take it so hard, I never would've—"

"How did you *think* I was going to take it?" Jessica swung the door wide open and pelted

Josh with a hurricane of stuffed animals. "Gee, thanks, Josh, you sure are a thoughtful guy!"

Josh ducked just in time to avoid a box of tissues and a platform shoe that was aimed straight for his head. Jessica's weapons were becoming heavier and more dangerous with each passing minute. "I'll make it up to you somehow," he pleaded, blocking a flying dictionary. "Let's go away together the weekend after next."

Jessica picked up the wooden plank that served as the top of their makeshift coffee table. "Why would I want to spend the weekend with you after what you did to me? What do you take me for? Some kind of idiot?"

Josh cowered in fright, protecting his head with his arms. "Not at all—I swear!"

Jessica dropped the board. Jaw set and teeth bared, she stalked across the room, a look of pure violence burning in her eyes.

"Let's get one thing straight, Josh," she said in a menacing tone as Josh backed away slowly. "I never want to see you again for as long as I live!"

Chapter
Thirteen

Isabella returned to the apartment, carrying two cardboard boxes she had found in the hallway, grateful that Lisa hadn't returned yet from Danny's. She kicked off her wet shoes, thinking about all the things she had to get done before Lisa came back. *I hope I have time to do it all,* she thought numbly.

Rosie came bounding out of Isabella's bedroom and curled herself around her leg, purring softly. Isabella lifted the little black kitten in her arms, feeling the comfort of her fuzzy fur. "You're the only friend I have left in the whole world, Rosie." She kissed the top of the kitten's fragile little head, right on the white diamond-shaped spot between her eyes. "I wish I could cuddle you all day, but I have some important business to take care of."

Isabella set the cat down gently in front of

her food dish, then headed straight for Lisa's bedroom. Rosie seemed uninterested in food, chasing Isabella's heels into the bedroom instead. Isabella carefully closed the door behind her.

"This is something I should've done a long time ago," Isabella thought aloud, dropping the boxes in the middle of Lisa's room. It wouldn't take long for her to pack everything—she'd just throw it all into the boxes. Then she'd carry them downstairs, write Lisa's name on the cardboard in big letters, and leave them in the storage cages downstairs. Isabella would call a locksmith to come and change the locks and voilà, Lisa would be officially evicted.

Where do I start? Isabella looked around the room. For someone who had almost no possessions a week ago, Lisa had accumulated an astounding number of things. Perfume, makeup, clothes—even the clock radio on her nightstand—were exact duplicates of Isabella's.

There's something seriously wrong with this girl. Isabella shuddered as she headed for the closet. Clicking on the light, she looked above the rod crammed with clothes to the shelf above, piled high with shoe boxes. *When does she have time to do all this shopping? Between classes?* Isabella had a feeling that two cartons weren't going to be enough to hold everything. She probably should have hired a moving company.

Just as she was about to topple the stack of shoe boxes, Isabella noticed a small wooden box tucked away in the corner. It was the same one with the carved rose that she had looked at the day Lisa had moved in. Lisa had gotten very upset when Isabella had touched the box, as though it held many secrets. Lisa had made her promise that she'd never touch it again.

All bets are off, Lisa, Isabella thought, grinning evilly to herself as she took the box down from its perch. Nothing could tear her away from it now.

Isabella carefully eased the cover off the box and looked inside. "What's my answering-machine tape doing in here?" she wondered. That would explain all the messages she never seemed to get recently. Isabella trembled. Lisa was even more calculating than she thought.

Underneath the tape were several letters in yellowed envelopes addressed to a Helen Mueller. *Who is that?* Isabella wondered. Since theft was obviously one of Lisa's favorite pastimes, Isabella thought that maybe Helen was her old roommate back in New York. They were probably love letters that Lisa had somehow managed to intercept. Isabella set them aside, not taking the time to read them.

There were several photographs in the box. The first one Isabella looked at was of a small white farmhouse with an old gray barn behind it. The buildings were surrounded by fields of pristine snow. Off to the side of the property was a frozen pond, and just beyond that was the edge of a thick forest. The other photos were nearly identical, showing the house from the same exact angle, except they were taken at different times of the year. In the spring and summer the green fields were covered with lacy wildflowers, and birds gathered at the edge of the pond. In the fall brown-and-gold trees provided a rich barrier for the edge of the property.

Setting the photos aside, Isabella uncovered at the bottom of the box an old newspaper clipping. She delicately unfolded the fragile yellow paper. The bold letters of the headline chilled Isabella to the bone: Mueller Twin Found Dead.

"The elevator is still broken?" Lisa looked at the Out of Order sign with dismay. She wanted to get up to the apartment as soon as possible.

It looks like I have to take the stairs. Lisa pushed open the door to the stairwell. Her long, pale fingers clutched a bouquet of fresh wildflowers wrapped in paper for Isabella. Judging from the look of shock on Isabella's face when she had seen Lisa in Danny's arms, she definitely needed something to cheer her up. Lisa hoped a nice fresh bouquet of wild-flowers would do the trick.

Lisa took the stairs two at a time, her heart as light as her feet. The warm tingle that Danny's gentle touch had triggered lingered throughout her entire body. All her hard work was finally paying off. Soon Danny would be hers, she'd become a member of the Thetas, and Isabella would get together with Josh. The vision was so perfect and clear in her mind, like a full moon on a cloudless night. Danny and Isabella didn't understand the brilliance of her plan just yet, but Lisa was convinced they'd eventually see it too. Then she'd have Danny's undying devotion, Josh's respect, and most important, Isabella's eternal love.

The door to the fifth floor slammed shut behind Lisa as she walked past the storage closet in the hallway. She fumbled for her keys in her purse, anxious to give Isabella the flowers. It was too bad she was taking it so hard. Some people just couldn't see that everything worked out for the best.

Just wait, sis, Lisa thought as she slipped the key into the lock. *You'll be thanking me when this is all over.*

"Jessica Wakefield—I never thought I'd ever see *you* darken my doorstep," Alison said when she opened the door.

Jessica rolled her eyes. "Trust me, Alison, I wouldn't be here if it wasn't an absolute emergency." She looked around to make sure none of the other Theta sisters were around to witness such an historic event. To Jessica's relief, no one was there. "Can I come in?"

Alison stepped aside primly and waved her in. She seemed pleased at the prospect that Jessica might need her for something. "You're a sister, Jessica. You're always welcome to *my* humble abode."

Alison's emphasis on the word *my* sent a shiver of revulsion through Jessica. When the room had become available several months back, Jessica and Alison had competed fiercely to see who would get it. Alison had won, and judging from the haughty look on her face, she was glad to have the opportunity to remind Jessica of that fact.

"I love what you've done to the place," Jessica said, her tone heavy with false civility. The decor was as frivolous and overdone as Alison herself, complete with frilly lace curtains and a ruffled white canopy bed. The place reeked of potpourri and perfume.

"Didn't my decorator do a fabulous job?" Alison said with a smarmy grin.

Jessica's eyes widened in mock surprise. "I had no idea Mother Goose was moonlighting as an interior decorator."

Without batting a curled eyelash, Alison fluffed the bow in her hair. "That's all right, Jessica. I wouldn't expect a simpleminded person such as yourself to appreciate the elegance of old French lace."

An irresistible urge to hurl some sneering insult seized Jessica, but she bit her tongue instead. "I'm not here to have it out with you, Alison, so let me get right to the point." Jessica was about to take a seat in a chair covered with fake white fur but suddenly thought better of it. "I think we're both in a position to help each other out."

A sly smile warped Alison's thin, silvery lips. "This sounds quite interesting," she said, sitting down at her vanity. "Please—go on."

I can't believe I'm coming to Alison, of all people, for help, Jessica thought ruefully. *But then again, I never imagined Isabella would steal my boyfriend either.* A desperate situation called for desperate measures, and Alison was her only chance.

"As we both know, my candidate, Lisa, is going to win the Theta vote by a landslide," Jessica said, giving her long blond hair a confident toss. "It's guaranteed."

Alison laughed, her pointed nose high in the air. "That strange little girl? You must be dreaming."

"I've taken an informal poll, and I'm afraid

Lisa is the overwhelming favorite," Jessica announced with an air of authority. "But I know a way to get your candidate in too."

Alison raised a pencil-thin eyebrow. "How?" she asked cautiously. "The only way for a new girl to come in would be for someone to leave—"

"Or to be kicked out," Jessica finished.

A glimmer of devious delight glinted in Alison's cold eyes. "Who did you have in mind?"

Just as she was about to speak, the name caught in Jessica's throat. *Are you sure you want to do this?* asked a little voice in the back of her mind. Getting Isabella kicked out of the sorority was serious business. *It could ruin her college career,* Jessica thought guiltily. *It could ruin her life.* Just as she felt herself softening, the memory of Isabella and Josh together in the coffeehouse hardened her again. It was too bad if Isabella's world fell out from underneath her. She should have thought of the consequences before stealing Josh.

"I'm thinking of Isabella Ricci." The name left a bitter taste in her mouth.

Alison's eyebrows raised a full inch. "This is getting *very* interesting."

Panic hit Jessica suddenly with the full realization that she'd just crossed a dangerous line. Now that Alison was involved, there was no turning back.

"What did she do?" Alison asked snidely. "Borrow your lipstick brush without asking . . . ?"

"Never mind," was Jessica's icy response. "Are you with me or not?"

Alison nodded vigorously. "It sounds like a backstabbing good time. I wouldn't miss it for the world."

Jessica began to pace the floor, her heels sinking deeply into the plush white carpet. "The question is—how do we go about doing it? Isabella's always been one of the sorority's most active members."

"That's easy," Alison insisted. "Everyone's noticed how Isabella's appearance has slipped lately. We'll convince them that she's not meeting Theta grooming standards and she'll get the brush-off. After a while Isabella will just quit on her own."

Jessica pursed her lips thoughtfully. "And when the slot opens up, your candidate can take her place."

"Beautiful."

Jessica stood still. "There's only one small hitch," she said. "I can't be the one to convince the sisters that Isabella isn't up to par. It'll look too suspicious since we were best friends. You're going to have to do that by yourself."

Alison plucked a piece of white lint off her pleated skirt. "No problem," she answered. "I was hoping you'd give me the honor."

Now that the deal was done, Jessica had thought she'd feel buoyantly victorious, but instead she felt hollow and sad. She'd never expected her friendship with Isabella to end so bitterly. "We have an understanding, then?"

"Absolutely," Alison replied, shaking Jessica's hand. Her grip tightened as she drew Jessica closer. "Just tell me one thing," Alison said confidentially. "What did Isabella do that was so bad?"

Jessica wrestled herself free from Alison's hold and headed for the door. "It's none of your business."

Isabella's heart pounded against her rib cage as she studied the faded black letters of the newspaper headline. The article was nearly ten years old. It had been clipped from the local newspaper in Rochester, Minnesota.

Mueller Twin Found Dead

The body of Rosie Mueller was recovered today after a five-day search of the woods near the Mueller family's home. Members of the local police force as well as a group of neighbors combed the area for nearly a week, searching for the nine-year-old girl. The child's frozen body was found in an old water well that apparently had been covered with snow and dead leaves. The coroner's report cited hypothermia as the cause of death.

Mueller was reported missing Tuesday by her twin sister after the two had gone into the woods to play. Rosie Mueller is survived by her sister, Helen, and her parents, Gloria and Robert Mueller of Rochester.

Next to the article was a photo of the twins. They were hugging, their cheeks pressed close together. The girls were identical, with long, light brown hair and big eyes, except that the one on the right, Rosie, smiled brightly, eyes focused directly on the camera. The other girl, Helen, looked away shyly, her mouth curved into an awkward smile. Isabella was taken with Helen, certain that she had seen her someplace before—when suddenly it hit her. The girl was a chunkier, younger version of Lisa.

Lisa was Helen Mueller!

The article slipped out of Isabella's stunned fingers and floated to the floor. Lisa had lied about so many things—where she came from, her sister's death, even her real name. How many other things had she lied about? Why did she do it? Who was she?

Isabella picked up the stack of letters she'd found addressed to Helen Mueller and started to go through them. Just as she opened the first letter, she heard the faint sound of a key sliding into the lock. *Oh no*, Isabella thought with fright. *Lisa's home.*

"Move!" Isabella said in a hoarse whisper, shooing Rosie to the other side of the room. She shoved everything back into the box, trying to remember the order she'd found it in. *Were the photos on the bottom or on the top?* She piled the letters in, the newspaper article, and the answering-machine tape and closed the lid.

The kitchen door creaked open. "I'm home!" Lisa called.

Isabella's hands shook uncontrollably as she tucked the box in the corner of the closet shelf. *She's going to catch me. She's going to be angry.*

Clicking off the light, Isabella turned around fast and ran for the bathroom door. She'd forgotten about the cardboard boxes she'd left in the middle of the floor when suddenly she tripped and landed with a *thud*.

Isabella lay still for a moment, a paralyzing pain shooting through her hip. As the sound of Lisa's footsteps came closer, she knew there was no escape.

"Did you hear me, Isabella? I'm home!" Lisa set the flowers on the end table and sighed with exasperation. She then walked over to Isabella's bedroom door and pressed her ear against it. "Enough is enough—you can't ignore me forever!"

Lisa waited two more minutes for Isabella to come to her senses, but still there was no response. *She can be so stubborn,* Lisa thought. "Fine—have it your way," she shouted. "But you're going to have to come out of there sometime!"

Lisa was headed toward the kitchen to get a vase for the flowers when she heard a sound. It wasn't from Isabella's bedroom, but from her own. It was a dull *thud,* as if something—or someone—had fallen. Lisa stopped in her tracks, straining to hear the faintest noise. *Is Isabella sneaking around in my things? What if she goes into the box?*

The thought of Isabella breaking her promise detonated an explosive fury within Lisa. "You said you wouldn't do it. . . ." she barked through tightly clenched jaws. "You promised!" Her blood was on fire. No one ever touched the box. No one.

"Isabella!" Lisa screamed as she stormed to the door of her bedroom. Her mind was a raging storm, spinning and roiling out of control. There was no telling what she would do.

Shoving open the door, Lisa was startled to find the room empty except for Rosie, who was chewing the laces of Lisa's brand-new leather boots. Cautiously Lisa entered the room. She checked behind the door, in the closet, under the bed, just in case Isabella was hiding. But she was nowhere in sight. Everything in the room was exactly where she'd left it, untouched.

The swelling anger inside her ebbed for a brief moment before resurging again with the force of a tidal wave. Lisa's green-rimmed eyes glared ominously at the kitten, whose sharp little teeth were piercing holes into the leather.

"What are you doing in my room?" she shouted, yanking the boot away. "You're ruining my boots!"

Lisa grabbed Rosie roughly, and the kitten hissed, swiping a paw across Lisa's face. She dropped the cat, feeling the first shock of hot pain searing her cheek. Scarlet blood stained her fingers.

"You're going to pay for that, you stupid animal!" Lisa shouted.

Chapter
Fourteen

_____

Whew! That was close. Isabella hurried across campus, her lungs begging for air. Just seconds before Lisa had opened the door to her bedroom, Isabella had managed to escape through the bathroom and into the safety of her own bedroom. Once she was sure that Lisa was in her room, Isabella had snuck quietly through the apartment and out the front door. It had been a clean escape. Her only regret was leaving Rosie behind. *I'll go back and get her later,* Isabella promised.

Adrenaline pulsed through her veins, making Isabella feel heady. While there was no reason to keep running, she couldn't seem to slow down. She ran past the library, the student union, and the coffeehouse, then down through the quad. The fresh air fed her lungs and cleared her mind, helping her to sort through the information that burned her brain like an overloaded fuse.

Lisa is Helen . . . her sister didn't die at birth. How exactly did she die? Isabella wondered. The article didn't specify if it was an accident or if it was murder. Regardless of the circumstances, it was a tragic event.

It must've been terrible to lose a twin, especially at such a young age, Isabella thought with pity. *But why did she lie about it?* She could almost understand why Lisa acted the way she did—she must have desperately wanted her sister back. *But I'm not her sister,* Isabella thought as she headed toward the administration building. *And this girl needs serious help.*

"May I help you?" A middle-aged woman with short brown hair smiled at Isabella from behind the counter at the registrar's office.

"I need some information," Isabella said between gasps, holding her side. "I need the home address and phone number of a new student who just transferred here. Her name is Lisa Fontaine."

The woman wrote the name down on a slip of paper. "Let me check for you—I'll be right back," she said as she scurried off to a computer terminal at the back of the room.

Isabella leaned her elbows against the counter. She wasn't quite sure how to deal with the situation, but contacting Lisa's parents in Minnesota seemed like a good start. If they knew what kind of trouble their daughter was causing, maybe they'd persuade her to move back home. The sooner Lisa left town, the sooner Isabella's life could return to normal.

The woman returned, shaking her head. "Sorry, miss—there's no listing under that name."

She's probably registered under her real name, Isabella thought. "How about Helen Mueller? Could you try under that name?"

Once again the woman wrote down the name and went to the computer terminal.

Despite the trauma of nearly being caught by Lisa, Isabella felt slightly relieved. All along she was the only one who sensed that something wasn't quite right about Lisa, and she had been beginning to think that maybe *she* was the one who was crazy. But now she had hard evidence. Isabella couldn't wait until Lisa's secrets were all blown out in the open so Danny and Jessica could see Lisa once and for all for who she really was.

"Did you find anything?" Isabella asked anxiously when the woman returned. "Is there a Helen Mueller in the computer?"

"I cross-referenced it with all the SVU directories." The woman shook her head. "I'm sorry. There's no one here by that name."

* * *

When the storm clouds of Lisa's temper finally dissipated, she found a bright, sunny mood underneath.

"That's much better," she said aloud, peering over the edge of the balcony. Lisa brushed her hands together with satisfaction. Another job well done. *It's amazing how good it feels to get the little details of life out of the way,* she thought. Stepping back inside the apartment, Lisa closed the sliding glass doors just as the phone rang.

I wonder if that's Isabella, she thought, rushing to the phone. "Hello?"

"I'm so glad it's you," Jessica answered. "I couldn't deal with talking to *you know who.*"

Lisa twisted the phone cord around her fingers, feeling slightly disappointed. "What's up, Jess?"

"I was just calling to remind you that the Theta election is coming up soon. I think you should make an appearance today at the house just to say hi to a few people," Jessica said. "We can't afford to lose any votes."

"Hold on—let me check my social calendar—" Lisa clasped her hand over the mouthpiece of the receiver, waiting for several seconds. "It looks like I have an opening. I'll try to stop by."

"Great," Jessica answered enthusiastically.

Lisa sat down on the couch, wiping a bit of

dried blood off her fingers. "So, Jess, how are you holding up?"

Jessica exhaled heavily. "To tell you the truth, not too well. I'm still in shock."

"I know this is probably going to sound corny, but I believe that things happen for a reason," Lisa said solemnly. "Even though this may seem really devastating right now, in the long run it just might be the best thing that ever happened to you."

Jessica snickered. "That's pushing it, Lisa. If this is the best thing that'll ever happen to me, then I'm in for one miserable life," she mused. "But at least I have your election to focus on right now. It keeps me from thinking too much."

Lisa held up her hand, fingers splayed, studying her long, strong fingernails. "I'm just glad you have such a worthy cause to devote your time to."

"Don't let me down, Lisa," Jessica begged. "Make sure you show up today."

"I'll be there," Lisa promised, hanging up the phone.

The delicate shell that Lisa had so carefully hidden behind for years was finally cracking open, and the new Lisa was emerging. It was as if she had been kept in a dark, cramped metal box until one day someone lifted the lid and let the sunlight in. For the first time ever Lisa felt as if she was finally able to stretch and grow and breathe. For the first time ever she was beginning to discover the person she was always meant to be.

Gingerly she touched the picture frame near the phone, the one with all Isabella's friends. *You're my friends now too,* she thought. It was all too much for her to believe. Lisa's heart was so full, she was afraid it might burst with joy.

Lisa grabbed the apartment keys and was heading out the door when she suddenly thought about Danny. *What if he calls?* She was worried that he might try to contact her and there would be no way for her to get the message. Then she remembered the message tape.

I'll just pop that baby in and be on my way. Lisa sprinted to the bedroom and took the wooden box down from the shelf. Lifting the lid, she reached for the tape. Then all of a sudden she stopped.

Everything was out of order.

The article was on top, then the photos, then the letters. It was completely wrong. In a frenzy Lisa flipped through each item to make sure nothing was missing. *It's all here,* she realized, tears coming to her eyes.

For a moment Lisa entertained the idea that she had messed up the order herself—until she looked at the pictures. The summer picture was first. *It's the winter picture,* she said to herself.

The winter picture always goes on top.

"You were here, Isabella. You went through everything!" A dry, throbbing lump formed in Lisa's throat. *This can't be happening. You found out about me and Rosie.*

Lisa's body shook violently in a mixture of hysteria and rage. Her lungs felt as if they were about to collapse. *What if she tells someone?*

Isabella had to be stopped.

"Lisa's really fabulous," Jessica said, taking a sip of tea. She set the cup and saucer delicately on one of the end tables and smiled at Magda. "I know she'd make a fantastic Theta."

Magda nodded obligingly, her dark, silky hair falling in loose curls around her shoulders. "I liked Lisa very much when I met her, but we spoke only briefly," she said, carefully enunciating each word. "It would be nice if I could speak to her at greater length."

Jessica shot an inconspicuous look at Alison, who was sitting working on a needlepoint pillow on the other side of the room.

"She promised to stop by today, so maybe you'll get your wish," Jessica said brightly.

"Jessica's right," Alison answered without looking up from her needlepoint. "Lisa's a perfect candidate. You should see all the great things she's done to Isabella's apartment—she has such *taste*."

Magda's intelligent eyes narrowed almost imperceptibly. "Isabella has fine taste herself," she said carefully. "If you don't mind me asking, Alison, why are you endorsing Jessica's candidate when you have your own?"

Nice going, Alison, Jessica thought, picking up her teacup again. Calmly she sipped, wondering how Alison was going to worm her way out of the situation.

Alison put down the pillow. "Why, Magda, I'm surprised you think that was an endorsement. I was simply saying that Lisa's a nice girl. I have a right to express my opinion, don't I?"

"Of course you do," Magda said, looking slightly irritated.

"Not that that would stop her anyway," Jessica added snidely. Alison scowled. Jessica smiled at her innocently as if to say, *It would look suspicious if I didn't say anything,* even though it still gave her immense pleasure.

"Lisa would certainly make a great contribution to the sorority," Alison continued.

Jessica shot Alison a look of warning. *Don't lay it on too thick,* she thought. *Magda will get suspicious.*

But Alison was too preoccupied with the needlepoint to notice. Either that or she was doing her best to ignore Jessica. "In fact, I think Lisa is better than some of our current members."

210

A curious look came over Magda's face as she smoothed the lapels of her blazer. "What exactly do you mean by that?"

"Well, I just think that some of our current members aren't quite living up to Theta standards," Alison explained. "Well, maybe it's just a few of them. Actually, at the moment I can only think of one."

Alison Quinn, the queen of subtlety. Jessica's fingernails tapped nervously against the edge of her teacup. The plan to get Isabella ousted wasn't exactly coming off the way she'd hoped.

"Who is this person you're talking about?" Magda asked, her eyebrows wrinkling.

"My goodness, it's getting late!" Jessica exclaimed, jumping off the sofa. Both Alison and Magda stared at her, their conversation grinding to a halt. "I was hoping to see Lisa, but it looks like I won't be able to. Please say hi for me."

"Of course I will," Magda answered, still looking confused.

"Are you sure you don't want to stay?" Alison asked with a smug grin. "I know you have a definite opinion on this subject."

"No, thanks," Jessica sneered. "I'll leave the backbiting up to you."

Lisa rifled through the kitchen drawer until at last she found a pair of scissors. Opening her palm, she drew the cool steel blade across her hand. The blade was sharp, cutting cleanly into her skin with little pain. Lisa watched in fascination as the white line quickly turned to red.

Unrolling a piece of gauze she found in the medicine cabinet, Lisa looked at the sky through the glass doors. The dim light of late afternoon was beginning to fade as thick blue-black storm clouds rolled in from the west. Distant rumblings of thunder grew louder as a weather system moved in.

"It's going to rain soon, Isabella," Lisa said aloud as she wound the bandage around her hand. "You can't stay out there forever."

The bouquet she'd brought Isabella was sitting on the table, still wrapped. Picking up the scissors again, Lisa sliced through the paper that the flowers were wrapped in, her clawlike fingernails grazing the paper as she cut. *I guess it was a waste to buy these,* she thought. Her greenish brown eyes were hard, unimpressed by the beautiful flowers that had moved her only hours before. All Lisa saw before her were the remnants of a sister who'd betrayed her— someone she could never trust again.

"This one looks nice," she said darkly, plucking a fresh pink carnation from the middle of the bouquet. She held the bottom of the stem with her bony white fingers and placed the scissors just below the blossom.

With maniacal pleasure she lopped off the top of the flower like an executioner at the guillotine.

A bolt of lightning split the air, followed by a crack of thunder. The black mood was creeping up on Lisa again. It was coming in slowly, but Lisa knew it was there, oozing through the cracks, seeping into every corner of her brain. For years she had managed to keep it at bay, but now it was returning, and there was no way to stop it.

You did this to me, Isabella, Lisa accused silently, snipping the blossoms off two more flowers. *You let it come back.*

The first time Lisa remembered the black mood coming on was when she was eight, when Rosie brought home a perfect report card. *Mommy and Daddy were so proud of you.* They gave Rosie treats like they always did and told her that she was their special girl. But Helen had been bad. *You're the evil one,* Mommy would say. Helen had gotten in trouble in school again and failed all her classes. They punished her by locking her in the cellar, in the dark. *You never should've been born. You don't exist.*

Helen wouldn't give them the satisfaction of hearing her cry. She'd push the fear down hard inside herself, pretending the cellar was a castle in some magical land and that she

213

was a princess. The rats and the spiders were her servants. *And they lived happily ever after.*

Then one afternoon Rosie and Helen went into the woods to play. Rosie wanted to play hide-and-go-seek.

Once they were deep in the woods away from home, Rosie picked a slender pine tree as home base. "I'm hiding, you're it," she called.

"How high should I count?" Helen asked. Rosie always had all the answers.

Rosie's nose was already red from the cold air. "Twenty. Count slow. And don't peek until you're done."

Helen covered her eyes with her arms and leaned against the tree. "One . . . two . . . three . . . ," she counted out loud. She heard Rosie scampering around in different directions, winter boots breaking through the crusty snow. It wouldn't be hard to find her—all she'd have to do was follow the trail of footprints.

"Nine . . . ten . . . eleven . . ."

Suddenly there was a crunching sound, then the muffled *thud* of falling snow. Rosie shrieked. Helen stopped counting for a moment, wondering if it was a ploy just to confuse her. *Don't peek until you're done,* she'd said.

"Twelve . . . thirteen . . . fourteen . . ."

When she reached twenty, Helen uncovered her eyes. "Ready or not, here I come!" she

214

shouted. She looked down at the ground at the wild, misleading pattern of footsteps that Rosie had made.

"Helen! Help!" Rosie screamed.

Helen looked around but didn't see Rosie anywhere. Where was the voice coming from? Was she hiding in the trees? She looked up.

"Help! Get me out of here!" Rosie called. *She sounds scared.*

Helen's fingers were numb. She balled her hands inside her mittens to warm them as she followed Rosie's voice. Jumping over a rotted log and pushing aside low branches, Helen finally came upon a hole in the ground. It was a stone well, narrow and deep. The well had been covered with snow and frozen leaves. Judging from Rosie's tracks, she'd stepped right into it.

"Helen . . . ," Rosie whimpered when she saw her sister. "Lower a branch down here—you can pull me out."

Helen peered down into the well. She was barely able to see the top of Rosie's head in the darkness.

"There must be a ton of branches around!" Rosie cried, on the verge of hysteria. "Hurry up! It's scary down here!"

Helen couldn't stop thinking about all the times she had to stay in the dark, creepy cellar while Rosie had all the fun. She was glad Rosie had a chance to finally see what it felt like.

"Don't just stand there! Do something. It's so cold. . . ."

Helen reached for an overhead branch and was about to break it off the tree when suddenly the black mood came. It seeped into her mind and dripped down into her body like sticky, warm tar. It spoke to every cell, every inch of her. *You don't have to do it*, it said. *Make her suffer.*

Helen let go of the branch.

"What are you doing?" Rosie cried. "Help me out of here, Helen Anne Mueller!"

Helen took one last look into the well, then walked away.

Even after all those years Lisa could still hear Rosie's screams echoing in her head. *I only wanted to teach her a lesson*, she thought. Lisa was only going to keep her down there for ten minutes or so, just enough to scare her. But she started playing in the snow, dancing, running, having fun. She blocked out Rosie's wailing, and when the sun disappeared behind the trees, she went home. Every time someone asked her about the last time she saw Rosie, Helen would open her mouth to speak, but the black mood always took over, making her lie.

Now that Isabella had found out about her secret, it was coming back again. Lisa snipped fiercely at the last carnation, her scarlet mouth turning white around the edges. She gathered the severed flower heads in her arms and slid open the glass door to the balcony. It was starting to rain. *You can't stay out there forever, Isabella. You're going to get wet.*

A jagged lightning bolt flashed, and thunder cracked the atmosphere. The black sky opened, releasing heavy drops of rain. Lisa leaned over the railing and spread her arms wide, letting the blossoms tumble to the ground.

You're going to have to come home sometime, Isabella. Lisa closed her eyes, feeling the drops pelt her skin. *And when you do, I'll be right here waiting for you.*

Chapter Fifteen

"I'm telling you, Lisa isn't who she says she is!" Isabella shouted, blocking Danny's entrance into the dining hall. The rain was coming down harder now in cold, wet sheets.

Isabella still couldn't believe her luck. She'd been running all over campus in the rain, trying to get up enough courage to go and see Danny, when suddenly she ran into him on the path. To Isabella, it was more than just a coincidence. She took it as a sign that she had to tell Danny about Lisa's secret.

Danny stared at her, raincoat hood pulled over his head, hands shoved into the pockets of his jeans. He stood a few feet away from her, seeming almost afraid.

"She's not who she claims to be," Isabella repeated.

"Who is she, then?" Danny asked, without

seeming the slightest bit interested.

Cold rainwater dripped from the awning overhead. Isabella shivered from the wet sweatshirt that adhered to her skin. *Hear me out, Danny,* she pleaded silently. *Just hear my side of things.*

"Her name isn't Lisa Fontaine—it's really Helen Mueller. She's not from New York—it's Minnesota," Isabella explained. "She had a twin sister, but she died when she was nine years old."

Danny's detached expression remained unchanged. "What else did she lie about—her blood type?" He seemed aggravated as he tried to step around her to enter the building. Isabella grabbed his elbow and stopped him from going inside.

Don't you love me anymore? Isabella searched his eyes for some sign that he still cared but could find none. The eyes that were once filled with affection and understanding had become a dark void.

"You have to believe me!" she cried. "Just give me a chance, and I'll prove it."

Danny recoiled, shaking her off. "I honestly have no idea what has happened to you, Isabella. You've changed so much." A flicker of emotion quickly danced across his face. Was it sadness—or anger? "I'm starting to wonder if I ever knew you at all."

Isabella felt a strong need to be in Danny's arms again, to remind him of how wonderful it was when they were together. Without giving it a second thought, she reached for him. "I haven't changed a bit, Danny. Things have been crazy, that's all."

Isabella slipped her hands behind his neck and pulled him close. Before Danny could object, she pressed her mouth urgently against his and kissed him. Her heart leapt at the familiar feeling of Danny's soft lips. Warm tears coursed down Isabella's cheeks. It was like being home again. But Danny's body was as cold and unyielding as a marble sculpture. Isabella continued to kiss him, hoping to break down his resolve, but her affection was futile.

Isabella pulled away, choking back sobs of humiliation.

"Don't, Isabella," Danny said in a quiet voice. "I know what's been going on."

Isabella was stunned. *Why would Lisa keep her secret from me but tell Danny instead?* She stared at him through a veil of tears. "How much do you know?"

"Everything." There was a bitter tinge to his voice.

"If you know everything, then why aren't you more upset?" Isabella thought that Danny would be furious at Lisa for her deception. It seemed more likely that he'd want nothing to do with Lisa, but instead he was standing up for her.

"I'm completely devastated, Isabella!" Danny cried. "What more do you want?"

Despite the fact that he claimed to know all about Lisa's mysterious past, Danny still didn't seem to understand that Isabella had been right about Lisa all along. "I want you to come back to me," Isabella sobbed. "We had such wonderful times together."

"I think it's a little late for that," Danny answered.

The rain was coming down harder still, saturating the grass and pathways, causing little rivers to form on gentle slopes. Isabella used to think it was romantic when they were caught together in a rainstorm, but now it just seemed incredibly depressing.

"Look, Danny—let's have a fresh start. I'm willing to forget about everything that happened."

"How generous of you!" he scoffed. "Did it ever occur to you that maybe *I* wouldn't be able to forget?"

Isabella's throat tightened. "Why not?"

Danny rested his hands on her shoulders, his eyes boring deeply into hers. "Once trust is broken, it's very difficult to get it back," he said. "In our case I'm not so sure it's worth trying."

221

Too upset to speak, Isabella simply watched as Danny turned away from her and disappeared into the dining hall. *I guess that's it*, she thought. *It's officially over between Danny and me.* It was a good thing he hadn't proposed to her after all. Isabella would have been even more shattered to discover that Danny was an unfaithful husband.

Isabella walked back to the dorm, rain pelting her back and making her feel like an empty shell. Hot tears mingled with the cold raindrops that trickled down into the collar of her sweatshirt. With no proof and no one on Isabella's side, Lisa had won. She had taken just about everything that was dear to Isabella. *But at least I still have Rosie.*

Sullenly Isabella dragged herself back to the apartment. It didn't matter if Lisa—Helen—whoever she was—was still there. She was going to pack up her things, take Rosie, and get out.

Isabella walked up the front steps, rainwater squishing in her shoes. Flower blossoms were scattered everywhere. *Did someone get married while I was gone?* Isabella thought, puzzled. She reached into her pocket for her keys, her fingers grazing the diamond ring Danny had given her. Her heart felt as though it were about to crack in two as she remembered her birthday not so long ago. Now that it was over between them, there was no real reason to hold on to the ring anymore, but Isabella couldn't bring herself to part with it. The ring represented the last pleasant memory she had of Danny and their relationship. She would keep it close to her heart always.

Pulling her hand out of her pocket, Isabella felt her keys slip from her fingers, landing somewhere near the bushes on either side of the step. *Great—this is just what I need right now.* Exhausted, Isabella crouched down and looked through the shrubs.

That was when she saw it.

It was a tiny black fur ball, covered in rainwater and mud. Its body was bent at an impossible angle.

"Rosie?" Isabella called in a quivering voice.

Reaching into the bushes with shaking hands, Isabella touched the kitten's fur. It was matted with blood. She didn't move.

An anguished cry escaped Isabella's throat. "Oh no!" She clasped her hand to her mouth and breathed in deeply to ward off the waves of nausea that kept coming over her. *Rosie's dead. Rosie's dead.* A deadly chill crept down her spine. Lisa was more than just a liar. She was a killer too.

May you rest in peace. Isabella put the last handful of dirt over Rosie's shallow grave and placed a carnation blossom on top. She buried the kitten only a few yards from the apartment building, in the woods, so that the grave was out of sight but still easy to get to. It was one of the many pieces of evidence that Isabella was collecting against Lisa.

But the biggest piece is still in the apartment. Isabella brushed her muddy hands against the front of her soaked jeans. Her muscles were cold and tired. All she wanted was a hot shower and something to eat, then to pack all her things and leave in the morning. *I can't go in the apartment while she's there,* she thought, looking up at the apartment window. The light was still on. *She's insane!*

It was already dark and the rain hadn't let up. Isabella sneezed, feeling the familiar tickle of an oncoming cold. "There must be some-place I can spend the night," she thought aloud as she walked out of the woods. With a great sense of relief she remembered Theta house. They would take her in.

It was Alison who opened the door. A look of absolute horror twisted her features when she caught sight of Isabella. With her rain-soaked clothes and runny nose, Isabella knew that she probably looked pretty frightening.

"Hello there, Isabella," Alison said, glaring at the muddy patches on Isabella's jeans. "It looks like you've sunk to new lows in personal grooming."

She sure knows how to make someone feel self-conscious, Isabella thought with embarrassment. She ran her hands through her hair in a last-minute attempt to neaten up. "It's been a rough day," Isabella said with a sigh. "Is the guest room open? I need to spend the night here."

Alison firmly placed her arm across the doorframe to block Isabella's entry. Her jaw was clenched as if she were prepared for battle. "I'm afraid it's taken, dear."

"I'll sleep on the couch, then," Isabella said, trying to push through.

Alison leaned her whole body against the doorframe. "That won't be possible," she said in a smooth, talk show hostess voice. "We Thetas have standards. I couldn't possibly let you in looking like that."

Isabella bit the sides of her cheeks to keep the tears from flowing. Even in such a miserable condition she was too proud to let Alison see her cry. "I'd love to change into something else. I'm sure someone has some clothes I could borrow."

Alison recoiled slightly as if she'd just seen a snake. "Don't you have some friends you could stay with?"

"Actually, at the moment I don't." In spite of the chilly air Isabella's cheeks were burning with humiliation. "I have nowhere else to go."

"That's too bad," Alison said flatly.

Why is she being so mean to me? Isabella wondered. Of all the people Alison had taken issue with in the past, Isabella hadn't been one of them.

"I want to talk to Magda," Isabella said assertively.

"Don't bother," Alison snapped. "She'd say the exact same thing. We've all decided that you aren't projecting the right kind of image that we expect from our sisters. Perhaps you might want to start looking into a different sorority. How about trying for the Deltas?" She gave Isabella a once-over. "I heard they need someone to dispose of the trash once a week. I bet it's right up your alley."

Suddenly Alison's attitude made sense. *I bet Lisa's brainwashed them too.* Isabella's lower lip trembled. "Can't you at least give me something to eat? I don't have any money and I left my dining hall card at home."

"Sorry," Alison said coldly. "And if I were you, I wouldn't go around knocking on people's doors looking like that. It's so tacky." She slammed the door in her face.

Crushed, Isabella burst into tears. *I have nowhere to go.* The cold, wet air felt as if it were seeping deeper into her bones, and her stomach growled for food. *This is it*, Isabella thought. *I'm going to die out here.*

Early the next morning Lisa woke up on the couch to the sound of the phone ringing. She was still dressed in the miniskirt and white blouse she had worn the day before. Sometime during the night, while she'd stayed up waiting for Isabella, she had nodded off.

"Hello?" Lisa said groggily.

"How come you didn't go to Theta house yesterday? I thought you were going to do some campaigning." It was Jessica. She sounded as if she'd been up for hours.

Lisa yawned and rubbed her blurry eyes. "I'm sorry—something came up." Isabella's bedroom door was still open. She had never come home last night. "You haven't heard from Isabella, have you?"

"I just talked to Alison," Jessica answered. "Apparently she went to Theta house last night to spend the night, but Alison turned her away. She said Isabella was a total mess."

Lisa's greenish brown eyes narrowed. *I should've known*, she thought darkly. *Isabella's running around campus telling everyone my secrets.* She dug her red talons deep into the sofa cushions. "You haven't spoken to her personally, have you?"

Jessica snickered. "Are you kidding? You think I'd talk to that two-timing loser?"

Lisa's bony fingers clenched the phone until

her knuckles turned white. "She's spreading lies about me, Jessica. She may have even reached some of the sisters by now. You can't believe anything she says." Lisa's voice was deep and gravelly. "Between you and me, I think she's gone completely insane."

"There's no doubt in my mind," Jessica replied tartly. "Aren't you sorry you moved in with such a nut?"

Lisa's fingers gently caressed the translucent skin of her pale throat. When she closed her eyes, all she could see was an inky blackness closing in. "Life can be strange sometimes," she said.

"Don't worry about the sisters. I'll make sure they know the truth," Jessica said. "In the meantime, you get over—"

Lisa hung up the phone before Jessica finished. She hugged herself, rocking back and forth, deciding what to do next. No doubt Isabella had make several attempts to tell people about her past. The sticky black mood was gushing in again, this time with the force of a hurricane.

"You won't get away with it, Isabella," Lisa hissed. "This time I'm going to shut you up for good."

Chapter
Sixteen

Where am I? Isabella's cheek was pressed against something smooth and soft—*leather*. Slowly she opened her eyes and blinked a few times. People rushed by, a few of them looking at her with disapproving glances. When her vision cleared, she spotted the wall of mailboxes several feet away. *I'm in the student union.*

Isabella swung her legs around and sat up, her muscles aching. The events of the previous day came crushing down on her like an avalanche. *It's not a nightmare,* she thought. *It's all real.* Isabella sobbed quietly as she remembered Danny's cold eyes, the Thetas rejecting her, and of course Rosie—it was all too painful to think about.

"It looks like someone had a little too much to drink last night," a stranger whispered loudly to the person she was walking with.

The stares and rude comments bounced off Isabella, wearing her heartache like a shield. She'd been through it all—nothing else could possibly hurt her.

Isabella struggled to stand up. Her body was stiff and her clothes were still damp. The burning sensation in her stomach reminded her that she hadn't eaten for nearly twenty-four hours. But the physical discomfort couldn't even compare to the pain that was in her heart.

Isabella slipped out the back door, praying she wouldn't run into anyone she knew. The bright sunlight blinded her, and even though it was warm on the surface of her body, deep beneath her skin the chill was still there. She shivered convulsively, certain that a fever was coming on.

Did Lisa leave the apartment yet? In the distance Isabella looked toward the window to their apartment. The morning sun reflected brightly against the glass, making it impossible to tell if it was safe for her to go in. *I have to get in there one last time—I need that box.* It was already too late to change Jessica or Danny's mind about things, but there was always the chance that the police might listen to what Isabella had to say. If nothing else, they could charge Lisa with cruelty to animals. Isabella hid herself behind the

Dumpster on the side of the building, waiting for Lisa to come out.

And finally she did. Dressed in a wrap-around floral skirt, white bodysuit, jean jacket, and high heels, Lisa strutted out of the apartment building, sliding a pair of designer sunglasses on her face. On the outside, she was the perfect picture of confidence and class, but on the inside, Isabella knew that ice ran through her veins.

"It's show time," Isabella whispered to herself as Lisa walked away. Stealthily she moved from behind the Dumpster and entered the vestibule of the building, careful not to be seen. She had to hurry—there was no telling how much time she had before Lisa returned.

The Out of Order sign was gone from the elevator, but Isabella decided to take the stairs anyway just in case. A rush of adrenaline hit her as she climbed to the fifth floor, making her body feel stronger and lighter. *You're going to make it,* she thought, forcing herself onward. *It's almost over.*

As soon as she opened the door Isabella wasted no time. Running to her bedroom, she grabbed a small suitcase out of the closet. She filled it with a clean pair of jeans and a few T-shirts, her toothbrush, a comb, a dry pair of sneakers, the alarm clock, and her purse. There was nothing else she needed or wanted.

Everything reminded her of Lisa.

Isabella's dull gray eyes fell on the picture of Danny on the nightstand. She picked up the picture and gazed longingly at his beautiful dark eyes, soft mouth, and handsome face. *If it's supposed to be over between us, Danny, why don't I feel it in my heart?* The whole situation didn't make sense. What could Lisa have done to make Danny give up on their relationship so easily? Deep in her heart Isabella believed that as soon as Lisa was taken care of, Danny would come back to her. He had to.

She put the photo of Danny in the bag and cut through the bathroom to get into Lisa's room. To Isabella's relief, the box was sitting in plain sight, and all the evidence was still in it. *Almost home free,* she thought, tucking the box under one arm. She picked up the suitcase and headed for the door. *Lisa, your fun is over.*

Isabella threw open the front door and gasped in horror. Lisa was standing in the doorway, a crazed look in her eyes as she noticed the box under Isabella's arm. "Just where do you think you're going?"

Isabella's eyes were wide and her jaw hung loosely like a child with her hand caught in the cookie jar. Lisa smiled cruelly, pleased to have taken her by surprise.

"What a strange coincidence to find you

here," Lisa said as she shoved Isabella back into the apartment. Isabella was as flimsy as a rag doll, falling to the floor with the slightest touch. Her eyes were flat and lifeless, and her complexion had a slightly green tone to it.

Lisa locked the door. "I was just going to see my boyfriend, Danny, when I realized I'd forgotten to take my little wooden box with me." She stared at a dirty and wet Isabella. She was sprawled out on the floor in a very unlady-like manner. "You look absolutely *atrocious*. I bet that mop on your head hasn't seen a comb in days."

Isabella sat up slowly and handed the wooden box to her. "Here it is," she said in a low voice, struggling to get to her feet.

How pathetic, Lisa thought as she stood over her. Lisa folded her arms across her chest and tapped her shoe against the linoleum as she watched Isabella lamely attempt to stand.

"I was just borrowing it, but you can have it back," Isabella answered, picking up her suit-case. "I'll see you later."

"Not so fast," Lisa said, locking the dead bolt. "Where were you planning to go with my box?"

Isabella swallowed hard. "I do-don-don't know," she stammered. "It was so pretty—I wanted to hold it."

Anger erupted inside Lisa with the force of

a volcano. She drew back her hand and slapped Isabella hard across the face. "Liar!" she shouted.

Touching her red cheek, Isabella reeled backward. "You're the liar!" she shrieked. "And a murderer!"

"Don't ever call me that again!" Lisa screamed, her eyes glowing like molten lava. Towering over Isabella, she raised her hand again. Isabella whimpered and backed away. Lisa dropped her hand to her side. "That stupid cat deserved it!" she shouted, pointing to the red scratch across her ghostly white cheek. "Look what she did to my face!"

"Danny doesn't love you," Isabella spat.

"I'm *not* going to listen to this—" Lisa opened the cabinet under the sink and pulled out a rusted toolbox. Lifting the lid, she found a large roll of silver duct tape. But as she turned back around she saw Isabella diving for the door.

Isabella was just turning the dead bolt when Lisa grabbed her wrists and pinned them behind her back. "You're not going anywhere," she hissed like a serpent. Isabella struggled against Lisa's dragonlike claws as she taped her wrists together.

"You're not going to get away with this, you know," Isabella said. "They'll lock you up."

Lisa spun Isabella around and knocked her roughly against the door. "I've already been locked up," she said, slapping a big piece of tape over Isabella's mouth. "And even they couldn't hold me."

Lisa dragged Isabella to the living room and threw her onto the rug. She sat on Isabella's legs to keep her from kicking and taped her ankles tightly together. Now that she was in control of the situation, Lisa felt her good mood returning.

"You know I love you, don't you, Isabella?" Lisa said, staring into Isabella's glassy eyes. "You make me so mad sometimes, but everything I do is because you're my sister and I love you."

Isabella rocked from side to side, the tape pulling her pasty cheeks back into a creepy grin.

"I'm going to see Danny, so you'll just have to sit tight until I get back. I'll even turn on the TV so you won't be bored." Lisa turned it to a music-video station, then set the remote on the telephone stand. "I can't wait to see Danny—I'm going to give him a great big kiss. He's an excellent kisser, isn't he?"

Isabella's eyes watered. She was trying to speak, but the words were muffled from the tape.

"Save it for later," Lisa said with an evil

smile. "We'll have lots to talk about when I get back."

Enjoy watching the TV show, Isabella, Lisa thought as she headed out the door. *It's going to be your last.*

"I suppose it's what you'd call an *unofficial* resignation," Alison said with a smirk. She stood in front of the antique mirror in the Theta parlor, fluffing up the puffy bow in her hair.

Jessica stretched out on the couch, filing her nails. "So she didn't exactly *say* she was quitting."

"The puppy dog look on her face was enough to tell that she wouldn't be coming back." Alison twirled her organza skirt around her skinny legs. "I wouldn't be surprised if she left SVU altogether."

Jessica's upper lip curled in disgust. "Good riddance."

As she said the words aloud, there was a slight sorrow tugging at her heart. Deep down Jessica was sad that Isabella was gone. Since the whole situation with Josh erupted, she'd begun to really miss Isabella and realize just how much their friendship had meant to her before the terrible mess. The plan to kick Isabella out of the sorority was a mean one—purely a scheme to inflict as much pain as possible on her—and apparently it had worked.

But how can you repair a friendship once you've been betrayed? Jessica thought.

Alison took a sip of tea, extending her pinky in the air like English royalty. "I never thought I'd say this, but we make a great team. Two fiendish minds produce astounding results," she said. "What's our next venture?"

"There isn't going to be another one," Jessica said in a melancholy tone. "I'm retiring."

Alison pouted slightly. "That's too bad. Between the two of us we could rule this campus."

Jessica shook her head. "You're going to have to do it without me. I'm through with schemes."

A moment later Denise stepped into the parlor, her face serious. "Jessica, there's someone here to see you."

"Who is it?"

"Josh," Denise answered.

Jessica scowled. "Tell him—" She stopped short. The last time she saw Josh, she'd decked him with a dictionary without giving him a chance to explain himself. Maybe this time she'd give him that chance. "Tell him I'll be right there."

Setting the nail file on the end table, Jessica stood up and smoothed the wrinkles out of her blue rayon jumper. *Be civilized,* she reminded herself as she walked to the front door. *Outclass him by a mile.*

"Good morning, Josh," Jessica said politely. She tried not to notice how gorgeous he looked in his black jeans and crew neck sweater. "What can I do for you?"

Josh backed away slightly, holding his arms up in front of him for protection. "Are you armed?"

Jessica held her empty hands up in the air. "No weapons," she said. "Why? Do you have more bad news for me?"

"Not at all," Josh answered, smiling. "In fact, it's really good news."

I wonder what it could be? she thought, leaning with her back against the wall. "What is it?"

A wide, sexy grin broke over his face. "I called up my friend, and our plans are on again. We're going to the beach house this weekend!" he said excitedly.

Jessica stared at him, one eyebrow cocked. "Is that supposed to make me cheer or something?"

"Just think, Jess—you and me at the beach. I'll have to bring along some WSVU work to do late at night, but we'll have the whole day together to do whatever we want," he gushed excitedly. Jessica hadn't seen him this excited in a long time. "And I have a surprise for you—I'm renting a boat for the two of us!"

Is he totally out of his mind? This guy doesn't get it at all. Jessica took a deep breath and counted silently to herself so she wouldn't lose her cool. "What about Isabella?"

"What about her?" Josh's smile faded.

"Don't you think she'll be concerned that her new boyfriend is spending the weekend with his ex?"

Lines of confusion formed on Josh's brow. "What are you talking about, Jess? I'm not going out with Isabella. What gave you that idea?"

"I saw it with my own eyes," Jessica answered coolly.

Josh rubbed his forehead, as if trying to recall some distant memory. "I've only seen Isabella twice—the day you were there and the other day, when Lisa told me to go see her in the coffeehouse."

"Hold on a second—" Jessica remembered that day all too well, when Lisa seemed bent on taking her to the coffeehouse for lunch. "Tell me what Lisa said."

He puckered his lips thoughtfully. "Lisa found me after class and told me she saw Isabella sitting in the window of the coffeehouse, looking depressed. Now that I think back, it seems kind of weird to me, but Lisa kept insisting that I should go over and talk to

Isabella. So I did. Then Lisa asked if she could give you the note about canceling our plans," he explained. "To tell you the truth, that girl gave me the creeps from the moment I met her."

Jessica's spine tingled. *Could Lisa have set up this whole thing?* The more she thought about it, the more she realized how strange Lisa had acted in the coffeehouse. Still, doubts lingered in her mind. "But I saw you two holding hands," she said.

"I did put my hand on top of hers to comfort her," he admitted. "But I swear it wasn't anything romantic at all. I told Isabella that a part of me will always love her, but I'm not *in* love with her. Isabella and I both know that we've grown completely apart, and while we had a great time together in high school, the spark just isn't there anymore." Josh's smoky blue eyes pleaded with her. "In fact, Isabella and I just ended up talking about how wonderful you are."

A hard, sour lump formed in the pit of Jessica's stomach. "You did?"

Josh nodded. "Jessica, I miss you so much."

"I miss you too," Jessica said quietly, pressing her palms flat against his chest. "So let me get this straight—you're not in love with Isabella, she's not in love you, and you never cheated on me."

"That's right." Josh leaned toward Jessica

and wrapped his arms around her waist. Jessica tilted her head back and closed her eyes, enjoying the sweetness of his kiss.

When Josh started to laugh, Jessica pulled away. "What's so funny?"

Josh shook his head. "All this time you were mad at me because you thought I'd cheated on you, and I thought it was because I'd canceled our plans."

Jessica laughed. "I hardly think a canceled weekend is reason enough to throw a dictionary at someone," she said sheepishly. "By the way, did I hurt you?"

"Not too badly," he said, pointing to the tiny bruise on his arm. "I was only in the hospital for two days."

Jessica gently kissed the bruise. "I'll tell you what. Why don't we stay on campus this weekend so you can get your work done, and then we'll go to your friend's house another time."

"Are you sure?" Josh asked.

"Positive," Jessica answered. "I want you to enjoy yourself without worrying about your work."

Josh kissed the tip of her nose. "You're the best, Jessica," he said softly. "Why don't we go somewhere to celebrate? I promise not to take you to the coffeehouse."

It was nice to make up with Josh, but Jessica suddenly remembered that the ordeal

241

was far from over. She still had to make up with Isabella, and of course there was Lisa to confront. *Lisa, you've got a lot of explaining to do.* "We'll have to do it another time," Jessica said, grabbing her jacket. She gave Josh a quick kiss on the cheek. "Right now I have an errand I have to run."

Chapter Seventeen

Isabella struggled to breathe. She was lying facedown on the carpet, tape covering her mouth. *Whatever you do, don't panic,* said the voice inside her head. But it was difficult not to. Lisa was going off the deep end, and there was no telling what she would do next. *I have to get out of here before she comes back.*

Anxiety prickled the back of Isabella's neck. *Think. There must be some way to get out of here.* Every time she tried to come up with an escape plan, she kept picturing Lisa alone with Danny in his room. What were they doing? The thought of it made her absolutely crazy. *Stop torturing yourself,* the voice said. *You've got to focus.*

On the TV, colorful images flashed in time to the beat of a throbbing heavy-metal song. Sweat beaded her forehead as the fever came on. Isabella rolled onto her back and took as deep a breath as possible through her stuffy nose. *If only I could scream, maybe someone would hear me.* She tried to part her lips, but the tape was so secure that they were completely immovable. *There must be something I can do.*

She looked around. *What about the telephone?* It wouldn't be much good if she couldn't speak, but maybe if she dialed 911, someone could trace the call. Turning on her side, Isabella hooked her feet around the legs of the telephone stand and knocked it over. The telephone and answering machine came crashing to the floor around her legs.

That was when she noticed the phone had been disconnected. Isabella started to cry. She kicked her feet in frustration, and all of a sudden her big toe hit a long, thin object. Isabella stopped and looked down. It was the TV remote.

Then she had an idea.

Wriggling a few feet down to where the remote was, Isabella turned her back to it. Slowly she moved backward, feeling for it with her fingers. The tape was unyielding, like iron cuffs around her wrists. *You can do it,* she told herself. *Keep on trying.* After several attempts the remote was in her hands.

Isabella rolled back onto her stomach, head

facing the wall opposite the television. The remote was balanced on the small of her back as she felt for the volume buttons. When she finally found them, she turned the TV up as loud as it could possibly go.

Someone has to hear me now, Isabella thought. Tears of relief streaked down her face. *When you get back here, Lisa, I'll be long gone.*

"Lisa, what's wrong?" Danny asked again.

For the past five minutes he had been trying to figure out what was troubling her, but she hadn't said a word. Instead she just sat on his bed, crying.

"You must've come over here for a reason," he said, offering her a box of tissues.

Lisa wiped away a tear. "I had a huge fight with Isabella," she squeaked before breaking into sobs. She pointed to a long, thin scratch on the side of her face and the bandage wrapped around her hand. "Look what she did to me. . . ."

Danny's eyes bulged. "She physically attacked you?"

Lisa nodded innocently. "And she's been spreading terrible, horrible stories about me too. She's saying that I'm pretending to be someone else—or something like that. I'm not even sure what she's talking about." She looked up at him, her hazel eyes wet with tears. "Has she talked to you?"

Danny touched her shoulder consolingly and nodded. "But don't worry. I didn't believe a word of it."

"Is it finally over between you two?" she asked, grabbing another tissue from the box Danny had offered her.

"It is," he admitted, sadly shaking his head. "Isabella has a lot of problems, and I just can't deal with her right now."

Lisa dabbed the corners of her eyes. "I'm glad to hear you say that because, to be honest, I never thought you guys were a good match for each other," she said. "I pictured you with someone more like . . . me."

Looking down, Danny smiled shyly. "Thanks, Lisa. I'm flattered."

"Don't you think it's a good idea?" Lisa asked, her face lighting up.

"What's a good idea?"

Lisa moved a little closer to him. She put her hand on his knee. "You know—you and me getting together. I fell in love with you the moment I saw you."

Danny did a double take. Lisa's eyes sank deep into their sockets, full of expectations and demands that he had no intention of ever meeting. "You're a sweet girl," he started slowly, carefully constructing the words in a way that would do the least amount of damage. "But I'm not interested in having a relationship right now."

Lisa stared at him for a moment, seemingly unconvinced. She reached up, cupping his face in her hands. "I know you want me, Danny," she said hoarsely, her face only inches from his. "You wanted me that night I came in here while you were sleeping."

Danny swallowed nervously. "What?"

"Remember?" She spoke casually, as if she were recalling a movie they'd seen together. "You woke up in the middle of the night, thinking someone was in the room." She giggled slyly. "You were scared out of your mind until you realized it was me."

Danny remembered that night very well. "It was Isabella," he corrected. "She was wearing her trench coat and her earrings and her perfume."

"Come on, Danny—stop denying it. You knew it was me." Lisa shook her head. "What boyfriend wouldn't be able to tell the difference between his girlfriend and someone else?"

What is she talking about? Danny thought back to that night. It had to have been Isabella; he was sure of it. It was dark, but the silhouette looked just like her—but then again, Lisa and Isabella had similar haircuts. *I know it was Isabella, because she said . . .* Then he suddenly remembered that she hadn't said anything at all. Why didn't it strike him as strange at the time? Come to think of it, there were

247

many things about the encounter that were odd. But the idea of Lisa impersonating Isabella was too bizarre. *It can't be true.*

"You still don't remember?" Lisa said, almost sounding hurt.

"I remember, but I think you're confused," he said, inching away from her. The odd glimmer in her eyes was unsettling. "You must've heard Isabella talking about it and somehow thought that you had done it."

"No, it was me," Lisa said heavily. "Let me refresh your memory." Tilting back Danny's head, Lisa kissed his neck the same way she'd kissed it that night.

Danny threw Lisa off him and jumped off the bed. His heart was pounding against his ribs like a jackhammer. "What are you doing?" he shouted.

Lisa licked her lips like a hungry reptile. "What are you freaking out for? You liked it the other night."

Danny paced the floor, wringing his hands. He was sick to his stomach. "Why did you do it?"

"I knew you wanted to be with me," she said, slithering toward him. Standing behind Danny, she put her arms around him and ran her hands from his chest down to his stomach. "I just had to prove it."

"Don't touch me!" Danny yelled, pushing

her away. "Let's get something straight—I didn't want you then and I don't want you now!"

Lisa's eyes darkened, the colors shifting from brown to gold to green. She staggered across the room and leaned against the desk, seeming to gather her strength for another round.

Danny's head ached. Oddly enough, things that he couldn't figure out before were finally starting to make sense. Like the morning after his encounter with Lisa, when Isabella stood him up and Lisa mysteriously appeared out of nowhere. Then there were the dozens of phone messages he'd left that had never been answered. And of course the crazy things Isabella had said about Lisa. Now he could see that she'd been telling the truth after all. And he'd acted like a jerk. *Poor Isabella*, Danny thought guiltily. *I'm so sorry I didn't believe you.*

Lisa's face hardened. "I know you're in shock right now—"

"Where is Isabella?" he demanded.

"It's no use talking to her, Danny," Lisa said dryly. "She's not going to take you back now."

"Where *is* she?" he repeated, baring his teeth.

Lisa looked at him dully. "She was so angry when I told her about us—"

"You *told* her?" Danny was livid. If in fact Isabella had been responsible for the scratch on Lisa's face, he couldn't blame her.

"What else was I supposed to do?" She shrugged. "Anyway, she was so mad, she packed her bags and went home. Now it's just you and me. Should we go out to dinner?"

"You've ruined my life!" Danny shouted.

Lisa traced her red bottom lip seductively with the tip of her finger. "I know a romantic little place by the beach I think you'd like."

"Listen to me, Lisa, and listen to me good." Danny grabbed his car keys and his jacket and headed for the door. "Your little fantasy is over."

I hope she'll forgive me, Jessica thought as she ran through the front entrance of Isabella's apartment building. The elevator was already waiting at the ground floor, so she decided to take it instead of the stairs.

The elevator was an old-fashioned type, with an outside door that looked like a regular door and a metal cage inside. Jessica slid the metal gate open, stepped inside, swung the outside door shut, and then closed the metal door. She pressed the button for the fifth floor.

"Creepy elevator," Jessica said aloud. The exposed lightbulb overhead threw just enough light for her to see the painted floor numbers appear on the wall of the elevator shaft as the car slowly moved up. The elevator felt as if it were straining, moving upward in spurts, so that it seemed to bounce with every floor it passed.

Please, Jessica begged silently. *Just let me make it to the fifth floor.*

Jessica had to get to Isabella as soon as possible. What if Alison was right in thinking Isabella was so distraught that she'd leave school? Or what if she did something more drastic? Jessica would never forgive herself if anything happened to Isabella.

The elevator finally crawled to the fifth floor and stopped with a bounce. As soon as the car was steady, Jessica slid back the gate and turned the doorknob to the outside door. *I made it,* she thought with relief. Stepping out into the hallway, Jessica heard loud music blaring from one of the apartments—screeching guitars and thudding drums echoing down the hall. *Who would play music so loud in the morning?*

As she walked to the end of the hall Jessica began to realize that the music was coming from Isabella's apartment. "What in the world is going on?" she said out loud. Jessica tried the door, but it was locked. She pounded it with her fists. "Isabella? Are you in there?"

No answer. *Isabella hates heavy metal—*

maybe it's Lisa. Either way, Jessica was determined to get inside.

Reaching up, Jessica ran her hand over the top of the doorframe. "Yes!" she said triumphantly as her fingers found Isabella's spare apartment key. The top of the doorframe had been Isabella's favorite hiding place when Jessica lived with her.

Jessica turned the key in the lock and was greeted by a wall of earsplitting sound. *That's odd,* she thought as she walked into the kitchen. *Why is the TV blasting if no one's around?*

Jessica walked into the living room to turn off the TV and found Isabella lying on the floor.

"Isabella!" Jessica screamed, staring at the hideous silver tape that bound her wrists and ankles. Isabella's eyes were wild with fright, yet they looked relieved when she saw her. Jessica quickly turned off the television and gently removed the tape from Isabella's mouth.

"We've got to get out of here!" Isabella wheezed, gasping for air. "Lisa's insane! She's going to kill us!"

Jessica pulled the tape off Isabella's legs. But before Jessica could ask her what was going on, she felt the sharp edge of cold metal against her throat.

Isabella screamed.

"So I'm insane, huh?" Lisa's voice hissed menacingly in Jessica's ear.

"I've been looking all over for you, Lisa," Jessica said with a nervous laugh. She held her hands high in the air. "I just came over to see if you wanted to go to the sorority house."

"I suppose you think I'm stupid too." Lisa dropped the knife. Before Jessica even had a chance to reach for it, Lisa grabbed both of her wrists and wrapped them with tape.

"Not at all," Jessica said calmly, even though she felt a wrenching pain in her gut. "But you should know that whatever you plan on doing here, it's going to severely hurt your chances of becoming a Theta sister."

"Thanks for the news flash," Lisa answered.

Isabella and Jessica's eyes locked. Jessica had hoped they could communicate a silent plan to each other, but Isabella's eyes only reflected the feeling of hopelessness that Jessica felt herself. *I'm so sorry.* She needed Isabella to know that, just in case anything happened. Isabella nodded imperceptibly, as if she understood.

Lisa grabbed Jessica by the elbow and dragged her to her bedroom. "I hate her as much as you do, Lisa," Jessica whispered. "Let me go, and I'll help you out."

"I'll come back for you later," Lisa said, opening the door to the closet. She pushed

Jessica in and slammed the door shut. "In the meantime make yourself at home."

Jessica slumped to the bottom of the dark closet. She could hear the sounds of furniture being moved against the closet door. Terror rippled down her spine. *What's going to happen to us, Isabella?*

Chapter Eighteen

Sitting at the kitchen table, Isabella picked up the pen and wrote with a shaking hand. *I've lost my boyfriend, I've lost my best friend. I have nothing left to live for.* She stopped writing and put the pen down.

Lisa pressed the knife's blade harder against her throat. Isabella could feel the teeth of the serrated edge biting into her tender skin.

"What did you stop for?" Lisa tapped her claws impatiently on the tabletop. The white tendons in her neck bulged. "I said—*I have nothing left to live for and I want to die.* Keep writing."

Isabella sighed and picked up the pen again, trying to ignore the throbbing in her neck. *And I want to die.* She wrote the words slowly, buying time. Maybe there was a chance that Danny would come over—that *anyone* would come over. But deep in her heart she knew the odds were against her. As soon as she was done writing the note Lisa was going to kill her and would probably do the same to Jessica. While Isabella maintained a stoic exterior, inside she was sobbing, grieving her own death. She couldn't stop thinking about Danny and her parents finding the phony suicide note. They would forever blame themselves, while Lisa would come out unscathed. It wasn't fair.

"Good, good," Lisa said, examining the letter. "Now how about something along the lines of—*if only you'd believed in me, Danny, I never would've taken such desperate measures.*"

Isabella shuddered. "No one's going to believe I wrote this," she answered.

"Of course they will," Lisa seethed. "You've been a total wreck lately—and everyone knows it. Now *write.*"

Isabella picked up the pen again and continued the letter. A loud banging sound was coming from the closet where Jessica was trapped. It sounded like she was trying to kick the door in. *Keep it up, Jess,* Isabella thought. *Fight with everything you've got.*

"Help! Somebody help us!" Jessica screamed at the top of her lungs.

Lisa dropped the knife to her side. Her mouth was drawn into a taut, thin crimson line. "What does she think she's doing? I should've taped her mouth shut."

"Help! Call the police!"

"Shut up!" Lisa barked.

Isabella continued writing, wondering what was going to happen next. She watched Lisa carefully out of the corner of her eye, anticipating any sudden movements.

Jessica didn't stop. "Someone's trying to kill us! Help!"

In a fury Lisa stalked off to the bedroom, taking the knife with her. "You'd better shut up, Jessica! I'm warning you."

Isabella looked over her shoulder. The door to Lisa's room was open just wide enough for her to keep an eye on Isabella.

Now's my chance. I've got to try to make a run for it.

"Help us!" Jessica screamed.

Lisa seemed furious. She started throwing aside the furniture that she had propped against the closet door. "That's it, you little witch—I'm coming after you!"

Without a second thought Isabella stealthily headed for the door. She carefully slipped out, then ran for the elevator.

I have to get help fast. Her trembling hands fumbled to close the elevator door, then the metal gate. She pressed the *L* button for lobby, and the antique elevator car began its slow descent. Isabella's entire body shook as she touched the stinging cuts in her neck. Her fingers were sticky and warm and covered with bright red blood.

Hurry, please hurry. Pure horror struck her heart. What was Lisa going to do to Jessica? Tears of fright coursed down Isabella's cheeks.

At last the painted *L* appeared on the cement wall. Isabella was ready to dash out of the car the moment it stopped.

But it didn't stop. It kept moving downward toward the basement. In panic Isabella pressed the *L* button furiously. "Stop!" she shouted. Still it continued to descend. "Stop!"

Danny headed for the student parking lot, keys in hand. Many strange things had happened lately, but this last turn with Lisa completely unnerved him. He had thought it was a simple, clear-cut case of Isabella falling in love with an old flame, but now, as he searched the lot for his car, he began to realize that he had absolutely no idea of what had actually happened. Nothing was as it seemed anymore.

Danny was walking down the second row, trying to remember where he'd parked his car, when he spotted something curious. *It can't be.* He walked closer and examined the vehicle from all sides, confirming his suspicions. *What is Isabella's Range Rover doing here?* he wondered.

Didn't Lisa say that Isabella had left SVU to go back to her parents' house?

"Excuse me, young man—"

Danny turned around to see a middle-aged woman with salt-and-pepper hair holding a handful of pamphlets. *Great, a saleswoman,* he thought tiredly. *Just what I need right now.*

"No, thanks," he said, holding up one hand and shaking his head. "I'm not interested."

"I'm not soliciting," the woman said pleadingly. She held up a photo. "My name is Nancy Mueller. I'm looking for my niece."

Danny stared at the photo. It was a picture of Lisa. A memory flashed through his head of the day before, when he was standing in the rain with Isabella. She'd tried to tell him something about Lisa—that she wasn't who she said she was. Isabella had said some name, but Danny couldn't recall what it was.

"Is she missing?" he asked.

"Helen escaped two weeks ago from a mental institution," Nancy said. "Have you seen her?"

Helen Mueller. That was the name Isabella had used. Danny's heart sank. Isabella had known all along, and she'd tried to tell him, but he didn't believe her.

Now she could be in danger—and it was all his fault.

"I'm sorry, I can't help you right now,"

Danny said quickly as he started to run back toward campus.

"Wait—" But before the woman could ask another question, Danny was gone.

"I told you to shut up!" Lisa lunged for the closet door, pushing aside the nightstand she had propped up against it. Like the eye of a storm, black anger was swelling again, moving in fast.

"Help me! Someone help me!" Jessica was crying hysterically now, her voice hoarse from screaming.

Help me, Helen, help me. Rosie's voice echoed relentlessly in the chambers of Lisa's mind. Lisa covered her ears and squeezed her eyes shut, but all she could see was the black well against the whiteness of the snow. *Grab a branch, Helen. Help me out of here.*

"Somebody get me out of here!" Jessica screamed.

In a fit of rage Lisa slammed her fist into the door. Blood trickled down her pale hand. "Shut up or I'll kill you!"

Jessica stopped shouting, but Lisa could still hear her mournful sobs through the door. Lisa was turning around to go back into the kitchen when she noticed the empty chair.

Isabella was gone.

"Isabella?" Lisa shouted, looking around the

apartment. The front door was open slightly.

She had escaped.

Panic seized Lisa. She dashed out into the hallway, but Isabella was nowhere in sight. *You can't be far. I'm going to find you.* The elevator wasn't on the floor so she headed for the stairwell, her mood darkening by the second.

Racing down the steps, Lisa saw a black cloud in front of her, swirling and spiraling out of control. At the center of the storm was Rosie. *Please don't leave me, Helen . . . I'm scared.* Lisa's head felt heavy, her arms and legs weighted down by the inky blackness filling her extremities. Each flight of stairs pulled her down farther into the cloud until finally she was completely sucked into the storm's vortex.

I'm coming for you, Rosie. Lisa opened the lobby door. It was empty. Through the glass doors she saw no sign of Isabella. *You can't be far away.*

Then her eye caught a glimpse of the numbers above the elevator. It was in the basement.

Lisa dashed for the stairs.

Isabella slammed the elevator button with her fist, but the car wouldn't budge. *I'll have to take the stairs back up to the lobby.*

Shoving back the gate, Isabella stepped into the damp darkness of the basement. She ran through the S-shaped maze, taking a sharp

261

right past the laundry room, then a left. Her breathing was raspy and shallow. Water dripped onto her head from the overhead pipes, sending anxious shivers rippling through her.

"You're almost out of here," Isabella spoke to herself as she trudged on past the storage cages. "One more corner and then—"

Isabella heard the exit door creak open. She stopped in her tracks, fighting the urge to ask who was there. Holding her breath, Isabella listened carefully, certain that her heart would explode in her chest. *It's probably just the maintenance man,* she told herself.

Then she heard the footsteps. They were slow and cautious—not at all the sounds of someone who was there to fix a pipe or to do laundry. Each footstep had a hollow sound to it that was familiar to Isabella. *Italian made . . . leather pumps . . . with a two-inch heel.* Terror jolted her like an electric shock. It was Lisa.

"One . . . two . . . three . . . ," Lisa began counting aloud with each step. Her voice had changed from a gravelly hiss to the voice of a child.

I have to get out of here. In panic Isabella looked around, trying to find somewhere to go. The storage cages were locked.

"Four . . . five . . . six . . ."

The incinerator room and the laundry room were the only two places, but Isabella knew

262

she'd only be backing herself into a corner. Above her there were water pipes.

"Seven . . . eight . . ."

Right near the elevator Isabella remembered seeing the shiny metal rectangle of an air-conditioning duct suspended from the ceiling. *That's it.* She ran back to the elevator.

"Nine . . ."

Scrambling up on a nearby crate, Isabella crawled inside the dark, metallic tunnel and waited.

"Ten." Lisa's voice thundered down the hall. "Ready or not—here I come."

Chapter Nineteen

Oh no, I'm too late. Danny covered his face with his hands and cried. Tears of grief rolled down his weary face and onto the suicide note Isabella had left behind on the kitchen table. *I want to die,* the note said. *If only you'd believed in me, Danny, I never would've taken such desperate measures.*

Danny sobbed uncontrollably. The most beautiful, intelligent, wonderful woman he had ever loved was dead. And it was all his fault.

The door to Isabella's room was closed, and he was afraid to look inside. *But what if she's still alive?* he told himself. *You could save her life.*

Danny opened the door slowly, gathering all his strength to prepare himself for the trauma of seeing Isabella's body. *Please let her still be alive—I'd give anything to hold her again.*

Danny peered inside the room. To his shock, it was empty. He moved inside and checked her closet, then cautiously opened the door to the adjoining bathroom. It was empty. Then he opened the door to Lisa's room and walked in.

Strangely, most of the furniture had been piled against the closet door. It wasn't until Danny drew closer that he could hear muffled cries coming from the closet.

"Isabella! It's Danny. I'm here—" Throwing the furniture aside, Danny swung the door open. "Jessica?"

Jessica's face was streaked with tears. She was slumped in the bottom of the closet, her hands tied behind her back. "Danny . . . it's terrible—" she choked as he helped her out of the closet. "Lisa has a knife—"

"Are you OK?" he asked, pulling the tape off her wrists.

Jessica nodded. "Just a little shaken up, I guess."

Danny's head pounded. "Where's Isabella?"

"I don't know." Jessica wiped away the tears in her eyes. "They were in the kitchen—" She stopped to take a breath. "Lisa was making her write a phony suicide note. I screamed for help, and Lisa got mad. She came in here, saying she was going to kill me. I think that's probably when Isabella slipped out."

A weird mixture of relief and horror arrested Danny. There was still a chance Isabella was alive, but as the moments ticked on, Danny knew the chances were getting slimmer and slimmer.

"Where do you think they could be?" he asked urgently.

Jessica shook her head. "I don't know."

"Call 911," Danny ordered, heading for the door. "I'm going to go look for them."

"Where are you, Rosie?" Lisa gripped the knife in her hand. Her fingers felt cold. She wished she had her mittens.

Through the darkness and beyond the storage cages Lisa could see the edge of the forest, dusk falling in blue light on the snow. The temperature was dropping rapidly, and Lisa could see her breath in the air like puffy clouds. Water dripped from the trees above. It was almost suppertime. It was time to go home.

"Rosie, say something. How come I don't hear you anymore?" Lisa dragged the tip of the knife blade along the wall as she walked. Her heels clicked against the snow.

Night was falling rapidly beyond the laundry room. Lisa heard wolves howling in the distance. She began to cry. "Come on, Rosie, I'm scared! Stop playing games!"

*　　　*　　　*

Isabella watched Lisa pace back and forth through a tiny hole in the air duct. Lisa's shoulders were slumped and her arms swung at her sides, just like a child's.

This woman is a total psycho. Isabella thought back to the newspaper clipping she'd found in the rose box about the death of Rosie. Was Lisa reliving that day in her mind?

"Rosie—stop playing! It's time to go home."

Maybe she'll get tired of waiting and leave, Isabella thought. Her knees were shaking violently. The thin metal duct sagged under her weight, and Isabella had the terrifying fear that it would let go at any moment.

Lisa's scared, childlike voice gave way to a hateful one. "Come out!" she screamed.

Hold on—it's almost over. Isabella breathed in, taking too deep a breath, so that dirt inside the duct irritated her nose. A fierce tickle hit her suddenly, and she had the urgent need to sneeze. Isabella pinched her nose and took shallow breaths, tears in her eyes and sweat beading her brow as she fought against it. Finally the sneeze subsided. *You're home free.*

With extreme care Isabella shifted her body slightly so that she wouldn't breathe in the dust. But just as she moved, the ring that Danny had given her slipped out of her pocket and fell to the floor with a *ping.* . . .

Startled, Lisa looked down at the ring. "What's this?" As Lisa looked up to see where it fell from, Isabella jumped out of the air duct, crashing on top of her.

"Rosie!" Lisa screamed as she fell to the ground. The knife she was clutching slipped out of her hands and went skittering across the floor, sliding under the washing machine. A rush of energy shot through Isabella as she bounded to her feet, leaving Lisa clutching her side and moaning painfully.

"Don't leave me, Rosie . . . ," Lisa gasped. Her skin had a deathly pallor.

Isabella ran down the hallway and didn't look back. The sudden burst of energy gave her newfound strength as she raced around the mazelike corridors of the basement.

"Rosie!" Lisa screamed.

Isabella's head whipped around to see if Lisa was following her. Suddenly she slammed into someone. "Lisa!" she gasped.

"It's Danny," he whispered gently. "Isabella, thank goodness you're all right."

A flood of relief eased Isabella's raw nerves, if only for a brief moment. In exhaustion she slumped against him. "She's after me, Danny," Isabella breathed heavily. "Let's get out of here."

Isabella took his hand and was leading him toward the door when suddenly a metal pipe came smashing down on Danny's head. His eyes rolled back as he fell in a crumpled heap.

Lisa was standing behind him, eyes glazed over, holding the pipe like a baseball bat. She waved the pipe in front of Isabella threateningly. "I guess it's your turn now, Rosie."

Five squad cars from the Sweet Valley Police Department came to a screeching halt outside the apartment building, lights flashing and sirens blaring. Jessica ran out onto the front steps to meet them.

A tall man in a business suit and sunglasses came up to Jessica while the blue uniformed police officers followed in tow. "I'm Detective Desmond—are you Ms. Wakefield?"

Jessica nodded. "You have to hurry—they're in the basement!"

He pulled out a notepad. "Who exactly are you talking about?"

"My friend Isabella and her boyfriend, Danny—and Lisa," Jessica answered impatiently. "Lisa has a knife—she's going to kill them!"

The detective jotted down a few notes. "Now, just slow down and stay calm. What started the dispute?"

The police officers stood unmoving in two straight lines. *Don't they even care?* Jessica stared at them in disbelief. Instead of answering the detective's question, she spun on her heels and headed back into the building.

"Excuse me, miss—where are you going?" Detective Desmond asked.

Jessica looked over her shoulder and shot him a disapproving look. "If you're not going to save my friends, then I will!"

Isabella slowly walked backward down the hallway as Lisa loomed closer, metal pipe poised high over her head. "You were hiding in the trees," Lisa said.

Trees? Lisa was hallucinating, imagining that Isabella was her sister, Rosie. She remembered the article, how it had mentioned that the girls had been playing in the woods on the day Rosie died. *Maybe the only way to get to Lisa is to play along.*

"Helen," Isabella said tentatively, watching her reaction. She continued down the dark hallway, moving back through the maze. "Helen, why don't you put the pipe down?"

"No," Lisa said, pouting.

"Please? Do it for your sister, Rosie," Isabella said as they turned by the laundry room.

Lisa's lowered lip trembled and her eyes looked scared, but the pipe remained firmly overhead. "You've come back to hurt me."

Isabella looked briefly over her shoulder to

see where she was going. The elevator was only a few feet behind her. "I don't want to hurt you, I swear."

"Yes, you do," Lisa said in a childlike voice. "You're mad at me for leaving you in the well." Her eyes filled up with tears. "I'm sorry I didn't tell Mommy and Daddy where you were. I didn't want you to die." Lisa broke down, dropping the pipe by her side.

"It's all right, Helen," Isabella said gently. "I forgive you."

Lisa rubbed her eyes with the backs of her hands. "I wanted to teach you a lesson. I wanted you to see what it was like to be cold and alone and scared."

Cautiously Isabella backed into the elevator. Leaving both the door and the gate open, she pushed all the buttons. Still the car didn't move. "Why did you want to teach me a lesson?"

Lisa stood outside the elevator car while Isabella punched the buttons. Lisa stared deeply into Isabella's eyes, as if she were transfixed on some distant object. Her tears dried and her pouty lip retracted, showing her bared teeth.

"Because Mommy and Daddy always loved you. They hated me!" Suddenly she jerked the pipe overhead again and jumped into the elevator.

"Helen, don't!" Isabella crouched down, covering her head with her arms. The elevator started to move.

"They wished I was dead!" Lisa swung the pipe in the air, indiscriminately striking the exposed lightbulb overhead, smashing it to bits.

Shards of glass rained down everywhere, and the light flickered out. The elevator was engulfed in darkness.

There was a sudden clanging sound, as if the pipe had been dropped to the floor. Lisa was quiet. Isabella stood up slowly, uncovering her head, listening to the low hum of the elevator as it continued up . . . up . . . up.

"It's all right, Helen." Isabella's voice sliced through the darkness. She pressed herself against the wall, praying the elevator would soon stop. "Everything is going to be all right."

Then suddenly Isabella felt Lisa's hands encircle her throat, squeezing tighter and tighter.

"I think the door is this way," Jessica said, leading a few of the police officers and Detective Desmond down the stairs to the basement. The other officers remained in the lobby as backup. "I heard voices coming from down here."

Jessica opened the creaking door.

The detective pulled her aside. "Let the officers go in first," he said.

They drew their weapons and turned on their flashlights. The eerie silence of the basement unnerved Jessica, who had heard so much commotion before the police arrived. *Something bad happened,* she thought. *I can feel it in my bones.*

"We've spotted a body," one of the officers said. "Appears to be a man in his early twenties."

"Danny!" Jessica cried out. She ran around the corner to where the officers were crouched. Danny was lying on the floor.

"Head trauma, appears to have been hit with a blunt object," one of the officers said.

Jessica touched Danny's shoulder. "Is he . . ."

"He appears to be breathing," the officer said. "But we don't know how severe the head wound is."

Two other officers who had scoped out the rest of the basement returned to the group. "No one is down here," one of them said. "They must've taken the elevator."

Detective Desmond radioed the officers waiting in the lobby. "Call an ambulance," he ordered. "And send all your backup to every floor in the building. We have a killer on the loose."

Chapter Twenty

Isabella's lungs burned for air. *I'm going to die,* she thought as Lisa's crushing fingers strangled her. Clawing at the darkness, Isabella tried desperately to push Lisa away, but she didn't have the strength to fight anymore.

At last the elevator came to a halt. Grabbing her by the neck, Lisa shoved Isabella against the outside door. The old door gave way, swinging open and sending both of them flying into the brightly lit hallway of the tenth floor.

Lisa lost her grip and slammed into the wall. In a daze Isabella sat on the floor, coughing as the cool air soothed her lungs.

"I didn't mean to do it," Lisa whimpered. She cowered against the wall. "Please don't hurt me."

Isabella tenderly touched her neck, still feeling where Lisa's fingers had been. It was so strange to see a grown woman in a skirt and heels whimpering like a child. "I'm not going to hurt you," Isabella said.

"I'll be good next time," Lisa cried. "I promise!"

The outside door to the elevator was still open. From the hallway Isabella and Lisa watched the elevator car rise to the next floor. *Thank goodness someone's in the building,* Isabella thought. *As they're coming back down I'll beg them for help.*

"Don't leave me," Lisa said, clutching the sleeve of Isabella's sweatshirt.

Isabella knelt down beside Lisa and rubbed the top of her head. Lisa curled herself into a tight ball, as if she were trying to make herself disappear. "I'm your sister, Helen," Isabella said. "I'll make sure that no one hurts you ever again."

Lisa's sobs subsided as she lay with her cheek against the floor. Isabella took a deep breath and exhaled slowly, tilting her head back against the wall. *It's finally over,* she thought with numb indifference. Soaked and aching, she imagined herself as a soldier who had just pulled herself out of the trenches after a harrowing night of combat. It was too soon to feel relieved—it was simply good enough to be alive.

Suddenly Lisa sat up, startled. She looked around. "Do you hear it?"

275

"Hear what?" Isabella asked, her nerves on edge.

Lisa swallowed hard. Her eyes were wide. "She's calling me."

"Who?"

"Rosie," Lisa said, tilting her head to the side. "She wants me to go help her."

Isabella turned Lisa's head toward her. "I'm Rosie," she said, pointing to herself. "I'm here and I'm fine."

Lisa's hazel eyes were clouded. "She says she's cold. I have to help her out of the well." She stood up and walked over to the open elevator door. Then she looked down into the empty elevator shaft.

"Helen—don't," Isabella said calmly in spite of the anxious tingle in her stomach. Keeping a few feet away from the shaft, Isabella took hold of Lisa's hand. "Come back where it's safe. Rosie's going to be fine."

"No, she's not—she's going to die!" Lisa stood on the very edge and looked down into the darkness. "I'm going to help you, Rosie. You're going to be OK."

The damp smell of the basement wafted through the elevator shaft. In fright Isabella gripped Lisa's arm with both hands and tried to pull her away from the edge. "Get away from there—it's dangerous."

"Let me go!" Lisa whipped around and

276

faced Isabella, the heels of her feet teetering on the edge.

"Oh no!" Isabella screamed, holding on to Lisa's shoulders.

Lisa pulled back, yanking Isabella closer to the edge with her. "I have to help Rosie!"

A wave of nausea hit Isabella as she peered down at the ten-floor drop, only a few inches away. Isabella's foot slipped, grazing the edge. "No!" Isabella squealed in fright, clutching Lisa's arms to regain her balance.

Lisa fell backward, her feet sliding right off the edge. As she dropped, Isabella, who was holding Lisa's right wrist, collapsed to the floor, her arm dangling over the edge.

"Oh no! No!" Isabella screamed as inch by inch she felt her body sliding toward the shaft.

Grabbing one edge of the doorframe with her free hand, Isabella slid sideways and hooked her feet around the other edge. Lisa's weight continued to pull her down until Isabella's head was hanging over the edge.

Lisa didn't scream or move. She only stared up at Isabella with her haunting hazel eyes. In her eyes Isabella could see the years of pain, the lost childhood, the anguish of losing her sister. The trauma of Rosie's life had shattered her, splintered her so that she could never be whole again.

Isabella shifted her weight to one side to

gain more leverage. "Hold on, Helen. I'll get you out of this." She slipped another inch.

"I'm going in after her," Lisa said calmly. "I'm coming, Rosie!" Then she closed her tormented eyes and released her grip, falling into the black abyss.

"Thank goodness you're all right!" Jessica shouted as they reached the tenth floor.

Isabella was lying in a pale, shivering heap near the elevator shaft. She smiled weakly when she saw Jessica, greeting her with outstretched arms. "I'm so glad you're all right too."

Jessica held her friend close, crying tears of joy. "What happened?"

"She's dead, Jess," Isabella said thickly. "She fell down the shaft."

The police put their weapons back in their holsters and filed out. Detective Desmond lightly touched Jessica's shoulder. "As soon as you're done here, please meet us downstairs for questioning."

Jessica nodded, wiping away a tear. She turned back to Isabella and held her tightly. "I'm so sorry for the way I acted, Iz. Lisa made me believe something that wasn't true— I don't know why I doubted our friendship."

"It's all right," Isabella said tearfully. She dropped her head into her hands. "Please, just don't let it happen again."

Jessica shook her head. "I don't deserve to be forgiven so easily. I was terrible to you and I'm sorry."

"I know you are, and it really is OK," Isabella said. "I'm just glad to have you back."

"Me too," Jessica said with a smile.

Isabella looked around, her face suddenly growing serious. "Where's Danny? Is he waiting downstairs?"

Jessica hesitated a moment before breaking the news. "I hate to tell you this, Isabella, but Danny's in the hospital."

"As soon as the doctor says I can leave, I think you and I should take a little vacation somewhere," Danny said weakly. He winced, as if a sudden pain had hit him.

Isabella took the pillow from the empty hospital bed next to Danny and tucked it behind his bandaged head. "Just concentrate on getting better for now." She kissed the tip of his nose.

"No, really—I think we should go somewhere to forget all about this mess. I want to make it up to you," he said. His dark eyes were sad. "Maybe we could drive down to Vegas or Mexico or something."

Isabella sat down on the edge of Danny's bed. Twenty-four hours ago she never would have imagined that she'd be sitting with

Danny, talking about vacation plans. She felt so wonderful to be with him again, realizing that everything was finally going to work out. Knowing Danny still loved her made Isabella's spirit soar, but her heart was still heavy. It was a bittersweet reunion because of Lisa. Even though she had put them all through hell, Isabella still mourned her death. Lisa's life had been one big, terrifying nightmare she could never wake up from.

"I'd settle for pizza and a movie," Isabella said, holding Danny's hand.

Danny smiled. "You sure are a cheap date—why did I ever break up with you?" he teased.

"Because you don't know a good thing when you've got it," Isabella answered.

"You're right about that." Danny cupped Isabella's face in his hands and kissed her softly on the lips. He ran his fingers down the length of her slender neck. "Where's your necklace?"

Isabella blushed. "Long story," she said with a sigh. "I lost it somewhere in the basement. I doubt I'll ever find it down there."

Danny shook his head sadly. He opened the drawer to the nightstand beside his bed. "It's a good thing I have this, then," he said, handing her a small box.

Isabella lifted the lid. The sight of the familiar emerald-cut diamond brought tears to her eyes. "How did you find it?" she exclaimed.

"The detectives found it when they were combing the basement for evidence," Danny explained. "There's something I regret not doing when I first gave this to you." Danny took the ring from her and, holding her delicate hand in his, he slipped the ring on her finger. "Isabella, will you marry me?"

Isabella stared down at the fiery diamond. Before, there was nothing she had wanted more than to be engaged to Danny, but now she knew deep down that it wasn't the right time. There were still so many things they needed to do, so many things they needed to learn about each other.

"Not now, Danny," she said, touching his cheek. "But someday."

Danny kissed the palm of her hand and looked at her lovingly. "You know, I'm going to hold you to your promise."

Isabella smiled. "I'm counting on it."

We hope you enjoyed reading this book. If you would like to receive further information about available titles in the Bantam series, just write to the address below, with your name and address:

KIM PRIOR
Bantam Books
61–63 Uxbridge Road
London W5 5SA

If you live in Australia or New Zealand and would like more information about the series, please write to:

SALLY PORTER
Transworld Publishers (Australia) Pty Ltd
15–25 Helles Avenue
Moorebank
NSW 2170
AUSTRALIA

KIRI MARTIN
Transworld Publishers (NZ) Ltd
3 William Pickering Drive
Albany
Auckland
NEW ZEALAND

All Transworld titles are available by post from:
Bookservice by Post, PO Box 29
Douglas, Isle of Man IM99 1BQ

Credit Cards accepted.
Please telephone 01624 675137 or fax 01624 670923
or Internet http://www.bookpost.co.uk
or e-mail: bookshop@enterprise.net for details.

Free postage and packing in the UK.
Overseas customers allow £1 per book (paperbacks)
and £3 per book (hardbacks)